PRAISE FOR KC GRIFANT

Grifant's exceptional ability to lure readers down the darkest of alleyways is on full display. Here, the feeders become the food and the prey becomes the predator. You'll be mesmerized by her Tales of the Uncanny, and there will be no driver waiting to return you to safety from the Shrouded Horror.

— REBECCA ROWLAND, BRAM STOKER AWARD
FINALIST AND AUTHOR OF *WHITE TRASH &*
RECYCLED NIGHTMARES

Shrouded Horror is evidence of KC Grifant's total mastery of short form fiction. Grifant writes with a classical sensibility for plot and modern nuance in her character work, making this collection perfect for those wanting old-school scares with contemporary craft and style.

— TREVOR WILLIAMSON, PODCAST HOST OF
SLEY HOUSE PRESENTS

Shrouded Horror reads like a grotesque funhouse ride, you never know what's going to jump out and scare you next! A wide-ranging collection offering something for horror fans of all stripes, KC Grifant has a penchant for twisted tropes and inventive monsters. Maybe you've seen zombies shambling out of the shadows before, but what's this one doing with a blue balloon tied around its wrist? Utterly delightful.

— BRIAN ASMAN, AUTHOR OF *MAN, F*CK THIS*
HOUSE AND *GOOD DOGS*

KC Grifant's *Shrouded Horror: Tales of the Uncanny* is a veritable time machine. It will transport you back to a time when, as a young reader, you curled up beneath a blanket on your couch and devoured stories by R.L. Stine and Christopher Pike. Grifant's stories beckon you in with the seemingly innocuous crook of a finger and then propel you through fantastical worlds of terrifying creatures, all-too-real scenarios, and creeping dread. I found something new and exciting on every page. So curl up on your couch, steel your nerves, and let the weirdness in.

— TIFFANY MICHELLE BROWN, AUTHOR OF *HOW LOVELY TO BE A WOMAN: STORIES AND POEMS* AND CO-HOST OF THE HORROR IN THE MARGINS PODCAST.

KC Grifant's *Shrouded Horror* is a testament to why collections are my favorite way to digest horror. From the end of the world, to cosmic circuses, to visitors climbing down from the valleys of the moon, these stories are captivating in their weirdness, frights, and fantasies. A standout collection from a master of the short form. Dive in if you dare, but leave the door cracked just a tad. The path back home may not be the same road you began your trip.

— TIMAEUS BLOOM, EDITOR OF *HOWLS FROM THE SCENE OF THE CRIME*

Grifant's stories are deliciously wicked with flawed but interesting characters and are perfect for lovers of *Tales from the Crypt* and *Goosebumps,* or any story where comeuppance is a key theme.

— JR BILLINGSLEY, AUTHOR AND EDITOR, SLEY HOUSE PUBLISHING

Grifant expertly demonstrates her creative prowess in this diverse collection of haunts. From urban creepy crawlies, to survivalist, environmental, apocalyptic and sci-fi terrors, *Shrouded Horror* draws you in like a spider to its web, wrapping itself around you in its cold, wet grasp. Each story is uniquely crafted with similar themes of acceptance, resilience and empowerment amongst a backdrop of strong female protagonists and underdogs that'll have you cheering from the bleachers. This is a must-read for any horror fan.

— FRANCESCA MARIA, AUTHOR OF *THEY HIDE: SHORT STORIES TO TELL IN THE DARK*

Grifant has a knack for devising the uncanny and uncomfortable. She delivers scares and shivers with tight plotting and descriptive prose.

— HENRY HERZ, AUTHOR OF *I AM SMOKE* AND *I AM GRAVITY*

This collection takes so many of horror's favorite tropes and sub-genres and twists them into something new and horrifying. Regardless of what poisons you usually pick, there's at least one story in here that will feel like it was written just for you.

— TASHA REYNOLDS, CO-FOUNDER OF THE SINISTER SCOOP

SHROUDED HORROR

SHROUDED HORROR

TALES OF THE UNCANNY

KC GRIFANT

Dragon's Roost Press

Printed in the United States of America

Print ISBN 978-1-956824-32-2

Digital ISBN 978-1-956824-33-9

Dragon's Roost Press

2470 Hunter Rd.

Brighton, MI 48114

thedragonsroost.biz

To my English teachers.
Your encouragement and enthusiasm
for storytelling helped more than you know.

CONTENTS

INTRODUCTION

This short collection is the culmination of several years of work. Growing up, I loved *Goosebumps, The Twilight Zone, Tales from the Crypt, Are You Afraid of The Dark?* and other episodic storytelling where something goes deliciously wrong. The ability to tell a full story in a short space—often with a satisfying surprise or twist—impressed on me the brilliance of quick, powerful tales at a young age.

Short stories, like any creative work, act a little like time capsules, reflecting a certain period in life. "Better Halves" and "What Storms Bring", two of my most popular stories, capture the feeling of paradoxical isolation while in dense cities or being with family. They also encapsulate my time in New England, where a unique culture and harsh weather intermingle. "Vermin," "The U-Train," "The Night Call," and "Puddle of Comradely Despair," meanwhile, relay the experience of living in Manhattan as a 20 something-year-old, along with the deep anxieties of surviving solo as a young adult in an intense environment. And stories like "All Aboard," "From Sea to Shining Sea," and "Just Another Apocalypse" are manifestations of environmental and global unease.

Introduction

The stories in this collection are odd and offbeat, but they all share themes in which something is off about reality. Whether it's a haunted jewelry box, a subway ride gone curiously wrong, or a glimpse of something malicious behind the mirror, these tales explore what horrors may lie just at the periphery of our consciousness. It is a place where time and reality bend, and where we find our ordinary selves woefully unequipped to deal with the unimaginable.

The next time you find yourself alone, I hope these tales give you pause and make you wonder if something uncanny is about to reveal itself— if only you look.

-KC Grifant

VERMIN

"Screw this," I said.

Emma looked unmoved, her face ringed by a mane of furry hood.

"We have to be patient," she said. "You want authentic city pizza or not?"

The line stretched three blocks ahead of us, made up of tourists and locals waiting to get into what looked like, frankly, a hole-in-the-wall.

"Even my goddamn *soul* is cold," I declared, still a little high. "I don't want to wait anymore. Even if it is the best goddamn pizza in the city. Or Brooklyn, whatever. Let's go to a bar."

"I'm not leaving. But I'm also not waiting," Collin said. He was used to getting his way and had gone on about how his "best New York pizza" blog would seal the deal for his A in Media Studies class.

"We'll pay someone ahead to hook us up," Colin decided. "Emma, wait here. C'mon, Gary." He dragged me out of line and marched toward the pizza's storefront.

"Po's," I said, yanking him back. The two cop uniforms waited near the front of the line, too close for comfort given the excess of party drugs we had loaded up on for the night ahead.

As we beelined back to Emma, a guy shambled toward us, grinning under a Yankees baseball cap perched over earmuffs.

"Gentlemen. I overheard your dilemma." He pointed his cane at us, a flash of silver elegance against a torn windbreaker and layers of frayed sports scarves. "I can get you signature Grizili's pizza in under ten minutes."

Collin arched an eyebrow at him. "Go on."

"For forty bucks, you get Herb's special: I send a personal text with the order and pick up through a friends-and-family entrance you won't find on any city guide."

A particularly nasty gust of wind screamed down the street and we paused to brace against it. For a second I wondered if bones could get frostbite.

"Done," Collin said between chattering teeth. "I'll take two slices of pepperoni. Gary?"

"Excuse us a sec." I tugged Collin aside. "You're not thinking of going with some rando. You know he's hustling."

Collin hissed back, "You just went into a warehouse yesterday with some rando for blow and that worked out."

"True." I couldn't argue. "But if we get mugged you owe me."

"He can't mug us. You're twice his size. And forty bucks is so worth it."

"He could have a bunch of friends waiting."

"Well, they're gonna be SOL. That's the last of my cash."

Emma started shaking her head as soon as we filled her in. "Bad idea."

"We're cold," Collin said imperiously, "and have places to go, people to see—"

"People to *do*—" I chimed in.

"You can hang out here, Em." Collin curled his lip as if we were standing in a sewer. "Or come with us."

Emma sighed under the pierce of Collin's ice-blue eyes, her self-esteem visibly crumbling under the full force of his persuasion.

"Whatever," she said. "As long as I get a slice."

"We give him the cash after," Collin said. "And if he gets weird Gary will handle it."

"Sure, I'll protect your weak asses." Typical. Just cause I was big I was supposed to be the bodyguard. "As long as he doesn't have a gun. Or knife. Or pepper spray."

Collin rewarded us with a smile and waved down Herb.

"It'll be ready as soon as we get there," Herb said after taking our orders. He led us between two bodegas in a space that barely qualified as an alleyway and tugged at a boarded-up door next to a row of trashcans.

"Do tell, Herb, how you managed such a lucrative connection to Grizili's?" Collin said.

"My old girlfriend." Herb wrestled open the door, revealing a set of steps. "Cheated on me with one of the cashiers. To make up for it she introduced me to the friends-and-family route."

Bitterness made Herb's voice husky, reminding me of one of our dealers on campus who always insisted on hanging out and rambling on about his latest ex. We'd do rock-paper-scissors to decide who had to meet with him.

A shadow skittered along the wall as Herb plunged down the stairs through the doorway. Not the first rat I've seen, but this one looked big.

"Um, guys? Let's maybe get burritos instead," I said. "I'm not feeling this. Not at all." Something rustled in one of the trashcans. "Did this place pass food inspection?"

"This escapade will be perfect for my blog." Collin gave my arm a squeeze before following Herb.

"I am *not* going down there," I said.

"Don't wuss out now," Emma said. "I'm literally starving, and we've lost our place in line." She disappeared after Collin.

I groaned and shuffled down the steps. We turned on our cell phone flashlights to keep up with Herb through a tunnel just wide enough for two people to pass side-by-side. The walls were cement, spotted with moisture.

"Is there enough air down here?" I asked. My cell phone shone a shaky spotlight against the back of Collin's hat. "Ugh, how long will this take?"

"You know," Herb said, his cane flashing in the dim light, "during the twenties, gangsters moved products with an underground network. High use during prohibition. When people wanted to drink. Fornicate. Do drugs. Your basic gluttony all around." A hard curve to his voice made me think he had a bone to pick with anyone who liked to have fun.

"And now?" Collin said.

"Now the tunnel is strictly for eats." Herb laughed. I expected it to be raspy, but his chuckle sounded a little high-pitched, a little unhinged. Something moved from the floor up to the wall above his head.

"Fuck me." Collin backed up and stomped on my toe. "What the hell is that?" Three phone lights danced on the ceiling. A few feet above us, the edge of a tiny, furred foot disappeared.

"Bat!" Emma shrieked. We listened to it scamper away.

"Or rat." I fought the urge to run back through the door and into the subzero wind, which didn't seem so bad now by comparison.

"Weird things down here, aside from me." Herb rapped his cane against the ceiling. "Shoo. Gone now."

"What *was* that?" Collin asked, his normally cool voice pitched.

"*Vermin,*" Herb said with relish. "Population's out of control. Poison doesn't work. Traps don't work. It's a real problem. Above ground and below. Gotta contain them."

"Probably disease-ridden rats," Emma said. "I *hate* Brooklyn."

I was still thinking of going back to the door, but Collin and Emma had started to follow Herb again. My boot crunched into something—I glanced down. Black pebbles, like droppings, lined the tunnel path.

"No way will this end well," I muttered as we continued on. We had followed a psycho into a mobster tunnel for God's sake. Now that my high was entirely gone, I could see what a monumentally bad idea this was.

Emma moved in close and squeezed my arm. "You're hyperventilating," she whispered. "We got this." It was like freshman year again, the two of us looking for someone to buy us alcohol and getting lost in less-than-ideal parts of town.

"This pizza better be worth it," I whispered back.

"Mozzarella straight from Italy and unbelievable crust, according to reviews," she said. "So worth it. We've done way sketchier things."

I had to laugh at that. "Remember the drug run in Grand Central?"

"Oh my *God*," Emma laughed too, and Collin sniffed ahead of us, probably miffed at the inside joke. He didn't like to be out of the loop.

Herb paused and our laughter cut short. The cell phone lights bounced off the side of his face, making him look half formed and deranged. Like a guy about to go on a killing spree.

This was it. Collin sucked in his breath and Emma gripped my arm like a vise. I took a breath and tensed, ready to launch at him if Herb attacked.

"We're here," Herb said simply and pointed up with his cane, where three stairs led to another door. He beamed and ran a hand through his hair, looking for all the world like a pleased host.

"I smell it," Collin said just as the aroma of pizza hit me, particularly enticing after our adrenaline-fueled walk through the underbelly of the block. We hurried forward when Herb grabbed Collin's arm.

"Payment," Herb said.

Collin fished out two twenties from his jeans.

Herb rubbed the bills and pointed again with his cane. "Enjoy."

"Could he *be* any creepier," Emma whispered as we popped out into a small cement room, crammed with a broken fridge and shelves piled with empty boxes and random junk. I took a breath, welcoming the delicious scents of fresh bread and cheese and peppers, barely masking a musky odor I had come to expect in the city.

Collin looked at me, amused. "Claustrophobic much?"

"I am literally salivating," I said and gestured to a pizza box with the signature *Grizili's* logo on one of the shelves. Cheesy goodness, the epitome of a New York pizza, thin-crusted and packed with toppings. I took a massive bite, not minding that it burnt the roof of my mouth.

"So yum," I said through the food.

"Save a bite for me, geez," Emma said, grabbing her own slice.

"Herb?" Collin called. "Do we go out how we came in, or…?"

I turned to see what he meant. The outline of the door we had come through had no knob. Piles of small black pebbles lined the ground. The urge to flee came back tenfold and I was ready to book it, screw Collin and Emma and the stupid food blog.

"Damn dude," I moaned, the bite turning into a hard lump in my throat. "How do we get out of here? Hey, Herb?"

Herb's voice floated through the door, talking to someone. "Big and meaty, should last for a while and keep them occupied."

"Herb?" Collin said, louder. "What the hell. We can't get out."

"Containment." Herb's voice came through faintly. "Restaurants pay a hefty chunk to keep the vermin out of their kitchens, any means necessary."

"I am literally salivating," someone said above us.

Something moved overhead, but it took my eyes a second to register the sight. Dozens and dozens of furred creatures the size of birds squirmed against each other, covering every inch of the ceiling except for the light fixture. They looked like bats, but bats didn't have fat little arms with claws and long beaks and tails flickering like the antennae of cockroaches. Bats didn't turn in unison to stare with four —no *six*—eyes clustered on their faces, reminiscent of tarantulas.

Emma's scream sent a nail through my ear as Collin bolted, taking cover under one of the broken shelves. My feet rooted to the floor. A few black pebbles rained around me and I brought my hands to my head.

"Damn dude," one mimicked in my voice, its six eyes flicking left and right.

"Save a bite!" Another squawked in a trilling imitation of Emma.

Emma screamed again and turned to me in a panic as a few of the creatures flocked from the ceiling onto her head and shoulders. Her face exploded into a patchwork of red slashes, claws and beaks blurring faster than I could see.

"Shit!" I screamed. I grabbed the closest thing to me—a handful of the light bulbs in a box—and hurled it, but the creatures didn't pause.

Emma fell with a shriek, furred bodies covering her in a mass of tails and muffling her cries. More of the creatures appeared through a small hole in the ceiling as the heady smell of pizza gave way to a stomach-turning stench.

Collin gestured to me from his hiding spot under the shelf, gripping a piece of piping. I started toward him but two of the creatures swooped dangerously close to my face. I turned and pounded on the door with all my strength.

"Herb! Jesus Christ!" I screamed. "Herb, let us out!"

The door didn't budge.

"Gotta control the vermin," Herb said. It sounded like he was smiling. "*All* the vermin."

"We gave you forty bucks!" It was an absurd thing to say but rage and fear short-circuited in me. "*Asshole!*"

I whirled at a crash. The creatures rained down on the shelf above Collin, crushing it on top of him.

"Help me, Gary!" Collin panted, swinging his pipe. I froze, back pinned to the door.

The pipe connected with one creature, which sailed harmlessly into the air, flapped, and perched back against the ceiling, watching as a dozen others chittered and dug into Collin.

"Gary! Gary!" the creatures called over his strangled sobs.

I pounded on the door again until the first claws stabbed my legs and back, sharp as switchblades. I spun and staggered, tearing at the hot, squirming bodies.

"Let us out! Save a bite! Gary! Gary! Gary!" Their voices drowned each other out as their tails lashed into my arms, reeking of garbage and musk and piss.

Through my tears and the tufts of fur, I spotted one creature next to our pizza box. All six of its eyes, black as abysses, regarded me.

"So yum," it said before it jumped.

GIFTING

LORI KNEW she had found something special when the dented jewelry box showed her the wedding ring resting in the folds of its cushioned interior. It was her mother's ring, buried three years ago with the body.

She turned the ring over in her hand. The rose gold band, cradling a tiny diamond, was a piece she had always wished for, but her father insisted it stay in her mother's grave. Lori placed it back in the jewelry box, which she had found yesterday in the secondhand shop.

"Anything you want. I'll buy it for you," Robbie had said in the store, a pit stop after city hall. He placed a strand of amethyst beads against her neck. "Your wedding gift."

He was an ugly man, always on the verge of a heart attack despite his new pacemaker. Not that Lori had many options. Robbie was good to her, mostly—as long she didn't make him angry or jealous—so she hadn't protested when they eloped without fanfare, even though she had to squash a part of her that wanted to scream at the thought of being bound to him forever.

"I know you, babe, know you wouldn't want all the fuss of a 'real' wedding," Robbie had said as they waited for the city clerk to finish the paperwork. "Besides, who would we invite, your family?" He guffawed at that, and she pressed her lips into a smile.

He'll take care of you, Lori had reminded herself. And since he had been her landlord, she wouldn't have to worry about being evicted anymore, at least.

That's when Lori had spotted the dented metal box, wedged in the corner behind a 3-foot cowboy Santa in the crowded store. It was a little rusted but inlaid with shards of mother of pearl, all beneath a layer of dust. A red clearance tag fluttered from it almost urgently.

"That busted piece of crap?" Robbie shrugged. "If that's what you want."

At home, she had polished the box until it gleamed like ice and settled it on a crocheted doily on her bureau between two candles. Perfect. She lined up items in a row along its peeling red velvet interior. The pewter "L" pendant from her first boyfriend. A handful of nickel-plated rings. Her prize possession, the relentlessly sparkling cubic zirconia studs Robbie gave her after she accused him of cheating. And now, her mother's ring, like a belated wedding gift.

"How is this possible?" Lori whispered to the box. "Can you...do it again?"

Something about the box reminded her of a lounging, watchful cat. It was ridiculous that she was talking to a jewelry box, but she couldn't help it. As a kid, she had always liked chatting to her toys, a habit which persisted as an adult—saying "good morning" to her shoes or "thanks" to the coffee pot. It helped with the loneliness, a little.

Other things started showing up in the box each morning, things she had wished for the day before—pieces of jewelry on other people that had caught her eye. The latest addition would appear on top of the other treasures, as if an attentive lover had planted them there to surprise her. Tiny crystals in the ears of the perky mall cashier handing out perfume samples. Creamy pink pearls draped on the collarbone of a mom at the grocery store. A stacked silver snake ring on a fast-food attendant's finger.

Robbie would never think to surprise her like that, let alone be able to afford the jewelry, but she needed to be sure. She placed a piece of tape over the lid, to test the unlikely event he had an elaborate plot to replicate jewelry she had seen and drank a few Red Bulls so she could keep a watchful eye from her bed that night. The box never moved.

In the morning, she could barely wait for Robbie to leave so she could check the box. The tape was still intact, but a multi-faceted peridot ring in a nest of hammered gold greeted her when she opened the lid. It was the exact piece she had seen on the bank teller when she had gone in to check her nearly nonexistent balance. Robbie insisted on keeping their accounts separate still, despite them being legally married.

"You're like the freaking tooth fairy," Lori squealed to the box and stroked its side. It felt warm, like it had been next to a fireplace. She wasn't losing her mind—the proof was right there in front of her. "I don't know how you're doing this, but thanks."

She bit back sudden tears. Damned if an inanimate object didn't treat her better than any living person on Earth. The box was silent, as usual, but it felt like a close friend listening as she poured out her heart.

"Am I going to get in trouble?" she blurted. "Is the stuff stolen, or replicated or what? Actually, you know what? I don't care." She'd deal with it later if she had to. For now, she enjoyed how people treated her differently when she wore the ring, the pearls, the gold. How she *felt*. Like she could lift her head, look people in the eye. It made her think of life the way she would've liked it, the way it might've been if mom hadn't had passed so early. If she and her dad hadn't commiserated with endless boxes of wine and Buds.

"Keep going," she told the box.

Even though she tried to make sure Robbie didn't see, sometimes she forgot. He pushed back her hair one night before she remembered the crystal earrings were still in.

"You got a boyfriend on the side? I don't think that's very fair, Lori." He panted in anger and his cheeks turned the color of a garnet.

The box could give things but couldn't take them away. A black eye. Bruised rib.

Items aside from jewelry started to appear. Her sister Stefy's golden valedictorian rope. Her father's Soldier's Medal. Things she hadn't wished for—or didn't *think* she had wished for—but nevertheless made an ache creep into her chest. Both reminded her of when she was younger and still talking to her family, still *had* a family.

"Thank you," Lori whispered to the box, tears streaming faster than she could wipe them away. She lifted a stray brown hair from the valedictorian rope. Stefy's. She gripped the rope tightly in her hand. It was the real thing, not a replica. Why had she sworn to never speak to her sister again; why had she skipped her dad's funeral? The reasoning was blurry behind alcohol-drenched memories. Maybe she'd call Stefy to tell her she found her rope in her stuff, use it as an excuse to reach out.

"I don't know how to repay you, but maybe this will help," she said to the box. She emptied it out and glued down the peeling velvet interior. Carefully as a surgeon, she used a tiny hammer from Robbie's toolbox to gently straight the dent.

"There. Fixed." Lori felt inordinately pleased as she gave the box one more polish. It almost looked new and seemed to hum, reminding her of a stray kitten's purr. Before she could put it back on her bureau, the door swung open.

"Hey." The single word made Lori freeze. Robbie's voice slurred and spat—a combo that made it clear he was going to have a Bad Night. Therefore, so would she.

She looked at him, widening her eyes so she looked as calm and unaffected as possible, hoping it would rub off on him. "Hi, babe. What's up?"

He frowned, scanning her for something to be irritated about. His eyes fell on the box, and she resisted gripping it.

"What else do you have in there?" Robbie said. "More jewelry from your other men?"

He darted forward. She turned in time so that his hand shoved her shoulder instead of the jewelry box.

"Don't you touch it!" she shrieked and slid the jewelry box across the floor until it bumped into the edge of the closet.

Robbie blinked in surprise at her defiance before his eyes narrowed. "I don't know where this sass is coming from, but it's not really respectful, Lori."

Lori dodged his first swing but couldn't twist away fast enough. He grabbed her waist and they toppled onto the floor.

At least he had forgotten about the jewelry box. She held onto the thought as she weathered the blows.

The next day Lori woke up late, wincing at the bump on her temple, the stabs of pain screaming along her back. But now she almost didn't mind it, not when she had something to look forward to.

Robbie was gone, no doubt off to his shift hours ago. Lori shot up in bed, an icy lacework seizing her heart when she thought he might have taken the jewelry box.

But it was there, forgotten on the floor next to the closet.

She breathed a shaky sigh and limped over before pulling the box into her lap. Her phone buzzed. Robbie's work. She ignored it. Bastard wanted to apologize, he could do it in person.

Her smashed hand ached something fierce but after a few tries she managed to open the lid.

Inside the box sat a shining bit of metal the size of a large coin, stained in blood. She clamped a hand to her mouth. Bits of pinkish matter clung to the device, but she clutched it to her chest anyway, feeling a crash of relief that made her sob aloud. She had only seen the pacemaker once before, at Robbie's operation.

It was the best wedding present of all.

ALL ABOARD

THE CITY LIGHTS TEEMED, sending a flood of crimson and violet colors along the dirty harbor water.

Two dozen people crammed into a single boat weighed down with basic medication, food packets full of concentrated goop, ample sedatives, and a water-waste filtration system. Just one of many lifeboats of those that had been exposed, cast out, waiting as the latest pathogen tore through society and spent itself.

Maurice avoided the sedative—he wanted to be alert in case they capsized, or something went wrong. He also avoided looking at one girl in the boat, who wore her hair coiled in dreads gathered on top of her head, reminding him of Elle and making his chest knot up every time he glimpsed her. Most of the others around him sank into dazes, muttering occasionally. He squeezed his eyes shut, the question running through his head like a water hose he couldn't shut off.

Why me why me why me

His mind picked over hundreds of choices he'd made in the past, branching out like the intricate lacework of his grandma's tablecloth, or like the eddies of foam in the water around them. He had gone down this path, all his choices leading him to this godforsaken boat.

If only he hadn't gone to the store that morning. If only he hadn't gone down the produce aisle. If only his mask hadn't slipped. If only the exposure reader on his wrist hadn't blinked red, a warning.

If only if only if only

"You have all been exposed. One in your group carried the virus in," a Protection Officer had said through his face shield to Maurice and the dozens of people rounded up, right there in a roped-off area of the grocery store's parking lot. "You need to wait it out thirty-one days on a Q Boat before you can return, then you'll get your Orange Card."

"Can't we go to a room or a facility?" Maurice had asked. Being on a Q Boat was the pits—no power, no Wi-Fi, nothing.

"All full," the Protection Officer said. Though he was muffled behind his shield, his irritation came through clear as a whistle.

"What about sitting at home?" Someone else moaned.

"Can't guarantee you won't break the quarantine," the officer said. "No more complaints or I'll stick you with a fine on top of it."

Maurice tried not to think of Elle, who he'd just started to get serious with. Serious to the point where he had bookmarked a few rings on a jewelry website and imagined different ways of proposing. Was she sick too? Was she waiting for him? And his ma—he *definitely* couldn't think of her and how she'd be shuffling in her worn-down slippers back and forth in her apartment, anxiously wondering when he'd get back.

It was Maurice's first time on a Q Boat. Now, not more than a couple days in, they had seen two passengers on nearby boats dive into the water and frantically paddle toward the shore. From boredom, madness or fear of further contagion, Maurice had no idea.

"Happens all the time," said Neck Veins, who acted like he knew everything. He snorted. "They'll just be sent back out here, if they make the swim."

Maurice didn't remember everyone's names, so he had given them nicknames in his own mind, especially the ones who didn't drug themselves into stupors. Aside from Neck Veins and Elle Lookalike, there was Bug Eyes, Blue Eyes and Tired Eyes, Skeletor, Fake Tan and Flabby Man. So far, none of them had any symptoms nor the telltale purplish hue along one's cheeks, another of the virus' inexplicable side effects.

The water looked burgundy in the twilight, making him think of runoff chemicals, blood, toxins. He hated looking at the water but couldn't help it. The endless lapping waves gave him vertigo, making him feel like he was about to tip over and be swallowed by the depths.

"I miss my apartment," he muttered.

"It's only a few weeks." Sunhat Woman's voice rang high and hoarse. She said it every few minutes or maybe every few hours. She pulled one of the reflective emergency blankets over her bony knees. "We'll be fine. Just fine."

"O-M-G. You guuuuuys," Blue Eyes wailed, wringing the corner of her tie-dye dress. Maurice fought rolling his eyes. Blue Eyes and said everything that popped into her head with the full force of a drama student.

"Lemme guess, another shark sighting?" Neck Veins smirked. "You think every shadow in the water is Jaws."

"The *virus*, dude." Blue Eyes pointed at Maurice. Maurice's stomach seemed to drop to the bottom of the sea. His hands flew to his face.

"I don't feel sick," Maurice blurted and then realized Blue Eyes' chipped fingernail pointed past him—at Elle Lookalike.

The look of shame that fell over the woman's face made the rest of the passengers sit up and take notice. In the boat's solar-lit glow, Maurice could make out a faint streak of purple, like fruit juice, along her cheek.

Everyone in the boat scooted back from her.

"You. You got us stuck out here," Fake Tan raged. He jabbed an orange finger at her once, twice. "And probably infected us all too. I missed my daughter's baptism because of this shit."

"I didn't know…" Elle Lookalike stuttered. Her eyes were white orbs, rimmed with lashes longer than Elle's. Her voice was softer too, like a pastel version of Elle.

"How?" Blue Eyes demanded.

Elle Lookalike's voice got very small. "My grandpa. I had to take care of him."

"I got laid off because of this damn Q Boat," Skeletor said. Long shadows ran down his gaunt face.

Fake Tan nodded in agreement.

"I'm sorry." Elle Lookalike cleared her throat, not quite a cough. For a second, Maurice wanted to drape a blanket over her shoulders, tell her she'd be okay.

"Let's calm down. Have some medicine, maybe," Sunhat Woman said.

"I have a better idea. Let's get rid of her." Skeletor stood, sending the boat swaying. Some of the other passengers murmured.

"Quick, dude. Before she gets the rest of us sick, and we're stuck here longer." Blue Eyes urged.

It wouldn't be the first time someone had been cast out off a Q Boat. Maurice had read a few accounts before he was out here, but never thought he'd witness it firsthand. He froze as the shouts of the passengers and protest of the woman rose.

"Wait!" Elle Lookalike gasped as Skeletor, Neck Veins, and Fake Tan led the charge to push her over. "Stop! *Please!*"

The woman's eyes locked on Maurice. He couldn't move. He shrank inside of himself and a tiny part of him hoped they'd get it over with.

This can't be happening, the shrunken part of himself said. *You're watching a movie. You're dreaming.*

He couldn't do anything. There were too many of them. But surely someone else would step in.

"Help me!" Elle Lookalike screamed again.

Hands shoved.

Other passengers looked on, disinterested.

Help her. Someone.

Elle Lookalike went over easily, the glittering water splashing around her head. She choked and her hands flailed above the waves.

Maurice huddled in his blanket, making sure to cover his cheeks, just in case.

He watched the colors twirl on the water as they floated away from her screams.

TERROR ON THE BOULEVARD

"CUT! TERROR! ACTION!"

Kelsie blinked and resisted rubbing her temples, which beat to a drum of one-too-many-vodka-tonics from the night before. The lights triangulating around her in the second-floor apartment seemed to wash the mustard walls in a color reminiscent of leering smoker's teeth. "Did you say…terror?"

"What, Kels?" The director-and-writer-slash-producer, Campbell, ran a hand through blond strands flapping along his undercut. "You're doing great, OK?"

Though a year or so younger than Kelsie, Campbell had already won some awards and gotten an "in" at a big film festival, so when he grinned at her in a way that made her stomach sink, she forced herself to smile back. Campbell hadn't quite propositioned her yet, but his stare said it wouldn't be long before he implied it was expected, a condition of her employment. He'd wheedle and make it sound like Kelsie was the ridiculous one, the naive one, for thinking she didn't owe him a quickie. *Just a blow job, no big deal.* He'd say it like it was the most reasonable request in the world, just one of a billion such exchanges in Hollywood, consistent as the unrelenting sun.

She hated blow jobs.

"Let's take it from the climax." Campbell gnawed on his lip. "We don't have a ton of time to get this just right."

"Sure thing." Kelsie ignored the nagging hangover and tried not to let the smell of the musty carpet turn her stomach. She pursed her lips into the subservient but confident smile she had perfected over the years while she envisioned a chunk of ceiling falling onto his skull. It was a trick she used instead of gritting her teeth, one she had done since she was a kid—a mental game of fast-forwarding time until the person's moment of death. The visualizations always soothed her enough that her smile would come off as sincere.

You have a plan, she reminded herself. She'd skip drinking with the crew tonight, claim it was a migraine, and keep Campbell at bay for a few more days of filming so he wouldn't have time to replace her.

"Hold up, got a weird buzz in the background," the woman doing sound said. "This place is *definitely* haunted. I need a sec."

Hairs prickled the back of Kelsie's neck, and she heard it too—not quite a buzz, more of a trill, like a crow's caw, but remixed and garbled.

"Make it quick," Campbell said and spread his hands wide. "I don't want to waste a second of this. Do you know how many crews like us get to film at Birdwatcher Butcher's? Exactly zero."

He reminded the crew *at least* once an hour how lucky they were to get access. The apartment overlooked a street near Hollywood Boulevard that was part of the Murders & Mayhem tour and was off-limits to filming. But Campbell knew a friend's girlfriend's dad who owned the building and gave them an exception.

The place was perfectly hideous. One side with wallpaper sporting diamonds of mustard and rouge, the other walls the color of washed-out bile. Campbell had literally clapped when they entered to set up.

"You know, they said there was no pattern to how he killed," the cameraman, Joe, said while they waited. "Unheard of for a serial killer."

Kelsie nodded. She had read the production notes: Birdwatcher Butcher had targeted men and women spanning race, religion, income. Twenty-two in total. And Butcher had always left a feather. She had studied by watching real crime documentaries featuring past serial killers and their victims. *Easy stardom*, she had thought bitterly, watching solemn montages of the victims' photos splashed on screen as the narrators speculated why the killers had picked them.

"They found him in this very apartment, heart attack. Or they *think* it was him." The camera man smiled appreciatively at Kelsie in a not-quite-ogle. "You're rocking this lighting by the way, Kels. Not a lot of actresses can pull it off."

Kelsie smiled back like he was the first guy to ever compliment her. With her raven hair and glass-green eyes, most people treated her as pretty, *special*, as long as she let them believe they had a chance at boning her. As soon as she sent a "no thanks" signal he'd undoubtedly get passive aggressive, maybe even purposefully make her look bad onscreen. The trick was to feign slight interest, gently tease him at arm's length. Keep him guessing, intrigued but not rejected.

It'd be easier with Joe than Campbell. Not being the director, Joe knew he was lower on their little social pyramid, but after a few drinks, he'd be circling like a hyena eager for leftovers.

Joe leaned back from the camera and against the top of a bureau, casually flexing. He glanced at the hem of her sun dress, a blinding yellow that Campbell insisted she wear. "Your boyfriend coming out for drinks tonight?"

She almost laughed. *Boyfriend.* How quaint. "I haven't had a boyfriend since middle school. No time with filming schedules."

Joe nodded, smile spreading. "Ain't that the truth. We should hang out later."

Prick, she thought while she preened. She pictured Joe's eyes bulging as an aneurism took hold. He'd groan and pitch forward onto the coffee table, maybe bashing in the corner of his temple along the way.

She tapped her finger along the windowpane as they waited. Through the thick, sealed glass, partiers staggered on their heels, laughing in the night as they headed to the bars. Why the hell couldn't she find a single gig where she didn't have to bat her eyes and act like she'd be DTF? What was she doing wrong?

Her friends shrugged off her complaints as the way things went – sex was the currency she had to deal in. One by one, her friends had gotten burned out and left LA for good. Kelsie wasn't ready for that yet. Some people wanted love, others money. But she knew, ever since she had gone viral in a YouTube video that got her a commercial deal back in grade school, that she was meant for fame. She was so close to that pivotal moment, to the golden opportunity that would ricochet her up the echelon into real success, she could feel it in her bones. Maybe this Birdwatcher Butcher film would be it.

She turned into position as the sound woman gave the go-ahead and Campbell barked at them to begin.

"He's going to kill me," Kelsie whispered to the camera through the harsh lighting. She picked up the taxidermized robin they had gotten at a Goodwill and contorted her face into a look of horror.

"Birdwatcher Butcher...it all makes sense," she breathed. "And now that I'm here..."

She looked up at the rows of framed feathers—cobalt, mahogany striped, magenta—that the real Birdwatcher Butcher had collected. She took her time trailing fingers along the framed images on the mantle, black and white, mostly photos. They showed tree leaves, store fronts, nothing particularly artistic, but all were historic artifacts from the killer. Her gaze settled on the one that caught her eye during every take: a charcoal outline he had sketched of a billowy bird-like creature, one that looked like a cross between a plague doctor and human-sized vulture.

She was in the zone now. She could almost feel Birdwatcher Butcher studying her from the shadows, like a stilted stalker, biding his time, taking in her every action. She let a shudder work its way across her shoulders, imagining his cold fingertips touching her neck.

She opened a drawer, where a butcher knife larger than her head rested, removed from the plastic display case they had set aside for the shoot. One of his knives, all of which he'd named after birds. This one had a wide yellow handle with the word "Canary" painted on it in blocky black letters.

"I'm going to die," she breathed. She arched her eyebrows as high as she could and willed the start of tears to make her eyes shine that much more.

If only a serial killer would *actually kidnap me. Then at least I'd be famous,* she thought sourly. *And out of Campbell's sights.*

A few hours later, they wrapped.

"Great job guys. Tomorrow, we do the big wow moment." Campbell chewed on a bit of beef jerky and offered a piece to her. "It'll look amazing. Red splattered against your yellow dress, here." He pointed, the tips of his fingers grazing her breast. Kelsie kept her smile plastered on, willing him to choke on his jerky, his face to turn gray from suffocation.

They headed down to the street, Campbell already handsy. She bit back her impulse to shove him in front of oncoming traffic and instead made a show of stopping in surprise.

"Damn. Forgot my purse back on set." She had a plan, of course. She'd wait an hour before taking an Uber back to the hotel. The lobby bar would be closed by then so she wouldn't risk running into Campbell. In the morning, she'd tell them she had a migraine and had to sleep it off so there'd be no hard feelings. Easy peasy.

"I'll catch up!" Kelsie unwound Campbell's sweating hand from around her waist. "Can I get the key?"

Campbell pulled it from his pocket, held it up like a gift he would bequeath to her. He glanced at the others, half a block ahead.

"Meet in my room in a bit for some notes, cool?"

"Oh, ah," Kelsie stalled. "I might call it an early night—maybe we can talk at breakfast?"

"I really want to get through these tonight." His mouth narrowed before he smiled. Really more of a smirk. "I know you're super dedicated. A real professional. It won't take long."

Kelsie nodded and all but snatched the key, biting her lip to stop a scream of frustration She ripped up the stairs to Birdwatcher Butcher's apartment and threw herself onto the couch. The shitty single apartment fixture overhead flicked enough to make her headache rear up again. She turned it off and switched on one of Joe's small spotlights instead, enough so she could move around without tripping.

She'd wait it out. Maybe Campbell would drink enough, find someone else and forget about her.

While she waited, she scrolled her social streams. She had a few thousand followers here and there, but not enough. She wanted to scream to the world that she was here, *ready*. Maybe this film would be the thing, if she could just survive Campbell. She closed her eyes, rubbing her temples and willing herself to relax until her phone buzzed with a text from him asking where she was.

Think, think, think. There had to be a way out of this.

> got a killer headache. raincheck?

she texted with a sad emoticon.

> power thru

he replied,

> or I find actress who is actually dedicated.
> haha.

She couldn't shake the image of his smirk. She pressed her hands against her temples. She stood to distract herself and started pacing. She stopped in front of Birdkiller's desk. The Canary knife peeked out from the half-open drawer, its handle shining in the dim light.

She picked it up. The coldness from the handle spread through her fingers. She had held knives before, and guns, and always felt the same spark of power, of relief. That feeling flowed through her now but stronger. She lifted the Canary, imagining the blade crunching into Campbell's forehead. God, that would be so easy, wouldn't it?

But she wasn't strong enough. Big enough.

And it was a *ridiculous* notion. She dropped it.

If only she *was* stronger, a man—he'd never treat her this way. It wasn't fair.

Her phone buzzed again. Campbell, persistent as a dog with a bone.

> u still at apt? coming over now.

"Damn it," Kelsie said aloud. She could leave but she was just delaying the inevitable. And seeing what a hard-on he had about getting access to the apartment, of course he'd want to hook up here. Her nostrils flared and she pressed a hand to her nose. The air smelled pungent. Stale, but also like a pot of dirt had spilled.

Something rustled behind her. *That was fast.* She whirled around.

"Campbell?" she called. "You want to do foreplay, this isn't it, babe."

A pause swelled before a sound crackled the silence.

A trilling, low and vibrant. Like a bird.

"Hilarious," Kelsie snapped but her skin electrified in a way that made her suspect it wasn't Campbell. Shadows hovered, shifting from the single spotlight, and reflected traffic light in the bumpy window glass.

Maybe someone had snuck in, a tweaker or homeless guy. She lifted Canary and tested the weight of the blade in her hand. The sight of it should scare off a would-be attacker, even if she had no idea how to wield it. A surge of iciness worked its way into her fingers when she moved the blade in front of her. She crept toward the darkened bedroom where the sound came from.

"I *will* cut you," she warned and strained to see.

One shadow loomed tall and thin along the bedroom door. She glanced behind her for the figure that cast the shadow. No one.

When she turned back, the shadow had peeled itself off from the wallpaper.

It stretched upwards and arched toward her in the gloom. Black membranes anchored it to the darkness and clung to a machete-shaped beak.

"Cool costume, bro." Kelsie's mouth stumbled over the words. "That's some fancy special effects…"

The figure, easily seven feet tall, moved like no animatronics or puppet she had ever seen. It arched claws, sharper and thinner than her best eyebrow tweezers. Orbs of white light glowed in its eyes.

Her mind froze, not computing what her eyes were seeing as she backed up.

It was the shadow vulture from Birdwatcher Butcher's sketch.

"Wake up, wake up," Kelsie moaned, twisting the skin of her arm. Her phone was out of reach, still on the desk. She backed into the window instead. Sealed shut. She pounded on it with her free fist and screamed, a good, theatrical, blood-curdling scream that would've made any voice actor proud.

The shadow vulture watched in silence.

"What do you want?" Kelsie shrieked.

It gestured with its claws and for a horrible second she thought it wanted her to pleasure it. Then she realized it was pointing to the knife in her hand.

"Canary? Not a chance." She waved the blade in what she hoped was a threatening manner. "Whatever you are, I bet you're not immune to a fucking knife."

The shadow vulture tilted its head a modicum, like a bird in the zoo.

It started to speak.

"For you," it rasped. "Gift." What passed for a voice made her think of a crow trying to talk. She shuddered, for a second feeling like she was going to vom. The sound was worse than the silence.

Canary's blade vibrated in her grip. She tried to suck some air back into her lungs. She was for sure hallucinating, drugged or dreaming. Whatever the case, at least the thing wasn't attacking her. A good sign, maybe.

"Aw, fuck," Kelsie said. "What are you, Birdwatcher Butcher's ghost?"

"No." Its voice rattled like a wind shaking dry branches in the winter. "Your wish. I help you. I helped him."

"My wish?" she said faintly.

"Famous." The creature trilled the word like something naughty, sending a tremor down Kelsie's spine.

"You want me to, what?" The blade in Kelsie's hand seemed to thrum, eager. She started to shiver and couldn't stop. "Use this to kill someone? Not exactly what I had in mind for fame."

"Not one," the shadow vulture hissed. Shadows streamed up and down its figure in a waterfall of ink. "I help you. Stronger." Power emanated from it like a cologne, like something she could almost dunk herself in.

"What if I say no?"

"Stay obscure. Mediocre. Weak." The shadow vulture took a step, and she jumped back without thinking.

"*Forgotten.*"

It perched on arching clawed toes, its silhouette bleeding into the floor.

Her anger flared. Dream, or haunting or whatever this was, the anger felt good, a remedy against the fear. She seized it.

"You're just another asshole trying to use me," Kelsie declared. "Ghost monster or not, I'm sick of it."

"Fame," the creature said, almost in appreciation. "We, partners. You…*Perfect.*"

Perfect? *Finally,* someone saw it. Her potential. Even if it was a weird shadow creature.

"What's in it for you?" Kelsie tried to buy herself time to think. Her phone vibrated again across the room, probably Campbell.

"Feed. Fear. Food." The shadow vulture's beak snapped, greedy. "You help. Kill."

"I can't." Kelsie dug her fingernails into her palm. "I can't go around murdering people, that's fucking insane."

"Some people. Deserve it." Its head rolled around on its neck, too fast, its beak flashing.

"Like what, pedos? Psychos?"

The creature nodded once and breathed more words around her that filled the room:

"Movies. Books. *Fame.*"

You're not really considering this, she told herself. The stream of thoughts came to her, as unwelcome as a downpour. Ted Bundy. Jack the Ripper. Jeffrey Dahmer. Household names, names that lived through history. People loved serial killers. There were countless shows that dove into the minds and lives of famed murderers. They had *fan* clubs for God's sake.

She'd be in the history books. With movies not just starring her, but all about her.

She shook her head, snapping herself out of it. She'd also be *dead*, or in jail. At best.

"No way. Again. I can't just *murder* people. That sounds gross. And also hard."

"Help you. Stronger," the shadow vulture said. The Canary blade glowed briefly in the darkness. Her phone lit up and vibrated on the table.

"Why can't you do it yourself?" Kelsie tried to stop the chatter of her teeth.

The shadow vulture lifted a hand toward her. "Need host. Partners. We bond."

"So we kill only people who deserve it?" She admired Canary in her hand, its blade as sharp as the creature's beak. "And you'll make sure I don't get caught?"

She got the sense the creature would have smiled if it could.

Even if I do get caught, she mused, *I'd definitely get film options and book deals.* Maybe she could even have an anonymous social stream going, if she was careful. She'd have fans. Serial killers always did. There weren't that many women serial killers after all, especially not hot ones like her. And if she only targeted really bad people and was careful about her branding, she could be hailed a hero, a vixenish vigilante. Like Batman, but in a dress. They might even give her a freaking medal.

The staircase in the hallway creaked. She could hear Campbell's whistle through the door. Her heart quickstepped in panic at the sound.

You don't have to worry about him anymore, she thought, and her pulse slowed.

She nodded to the creature. "OK, let's do this bond or whatever. Quick."

The shadow vulture reached toward her and Canary. She winced, expecting pain, but when the pinprick of its claw touched her wrist, a flush of strength slammed through her, faster than a long snort of coke. Threads of gray shadows ran up and around her arm like lace, sinking deep into her skin and she gripped the blade tighter. A nickname rang out to her:

Canary Killer.

It was so perfect that she almost squealed, even as she heard the doorknob turn. The shadow vulture's power moved her muscles seamlessly, guiding her to step behind the door. Darkness folded around her so Campbell wouldn't see her until it was too late.

She held the knife against her dress, picturing the most Instagrammable angle of the chrome against a technicolor splash of Campbell's blood and the yellow fabric.

She'd get millions of followers, no problem.

And best of all—no more blow jobs.

JUST ANOTHER APOCALYPSE

WE CRUISE UP THE 5, zombies staggering on either side of the highway, their cerulean balloons straining in the wind like a flock of chained bluebirds.

At first it was a viral game, a way to rack up social media hits: run up behind a zombie and tie a balloon to them without getting bitten. Then it became a public service, helping people to spot an approaching hoard.

I try not to feel too bummed as we zip north. It's been a year or so since we've been dealing with this latest apocalypse on the heels of the last wildfires, which still left a persistent orange tinge on the horizon. I should be over it by now but something about the scene is bringing me down. How many kids would ever look at a balloon the same way now? I remember the pull of a balloon's thread at my wrist, tugging at it until I watched the orb float off into the night. When you were little, it was fun, simple. Why did humanity have to screw up so bad that yet another virus took hold, this one turning half the population into flesh-eating ghouls—real-life zombies?

"Yo Gus," Vicki says, pulling me out of my misanthropic musings. She and Madison are holding hands, a sweet gesture that makes me feel a little bit better in this hellscape. "Whatcha thinking about?"

Vicki has that chattery vibe she gets when she's nervous. With her free hand she's smoothing down her frizzy hair in the rearview mirror, tossing a clump of strands out the window. The stress affects us all in weird ways.

I strain to see the gas gauge for the umpteenth time. Maybe 40 miles of fuel left so we'll have to stop soon. You can't wait until the last minute on anything nowadays. Survival's all about prep and vigilance.

"Thanks again for picking me up," I say. If they hadn't deemed my hitchhiking ass not a threat, I'd still be stuck in Flagstaff, trying to fend off my former college roommate who tried to kill me with a lacrosse stick. "Kindness is like the only real currency nowadays, you know?"

I've been with them two days and it already feels like we've been friends for ages: we've dodged two hordes, met up with fellow transients for a bonfire in San Diego, and took a quick dive in the cold waters before heading up the coast.

Vicki stops messing with her hair and smiles. "So, you pick your final destination?"

"I'm thinking Seattle. There's still a coffee scene there I hear," I say and look away from the sea of balloons. We drive past busted-up cars, rows of encampments. "I learned how to make a mean latte in the before-times."

People still ate, worked, drank. If anything, demand for caffeine—and most other escapist services—had soared. Pretty much everyone got infected, and they estimate about a quarter turned into zombies with a taste for flesh. Those who recovered from the infection—a week in bed before their immune system successfully fought off the virus—are making do, going about their days, just with more caution. It wasn't all that different than before, just a little more dangerous, a little more unpredictable. A little more depressing.

"Once we get to the commune, we're going to start farming." Vicki's eyes widen in nervous excitement. "There's a microclimate northeast of San Fran that some people are having luck with."

They keep talking about some damn commune outside of Portland. They had invited me, but I'd rather get eaten alive ten times over than have to farm.

"Too damn hot in Arizona," Madison grunts. Her reflection isn't much better: her eyes are bloodshot and a cut along her forehead from our last horde encounter is red and blistered. Her glance slides over to the huge box crammed into the back seat next to me. Full of seeds and other farming shit.

"You'd be surprised how hard seeds are to get now," Vicki trails off. "God, I'm starving. Sorry."

As soon as she says it, my stomach shudders and groans like an abandoned puppy. The bonfire the night before last is a lifetime ago. It had almost felt normal again, meeting new people and hanging out. They had been happy to share BBQ and cans of beer.

"Let's try this one, kiddos." Madison points to a gas station sign and we all go silent, somber. Readying for whatever might be waiting for us.

We roll in front of a lit gas pump. Another car, empty and dark and the color of dried blood, sits at the second pump. Madison starts fueling—her credit card still works, one of those cryptocurrency cards —and the two of them go around to the outside bathroom.

I keep an eye out, perch on the hood between blotted rust stains. Through the barred glass windows of the station, the shelves are messy, no food, just packages of car fresheners and replacement windshield wipers, at least that I can see. I glimpse one attendant behind a bulletproof encasement, watching something on TV. A shotgun rests across his knees. From here I can't tell if he's a zombie or not.

The zombies are slow for the most part but not completely un-dangerous. They have enough cognitive skills to figure out basics – how to wield a weapon, communicate with each other, even how to drive a car in some cases. They like to travel in packs. Some of them act like toddlers, carrying around the equivalent of a security blanket, random objects they find on the street or on one of their victims. They're easily distracted by TV or phone screens, which was funny at first but now I just feel irritated at how stupid they are. Like, die off or be functional members of society, you know?

I finish scanning the scene and spot one zombie hovering on the opposite side of the gas station with that stereotypical bug-eyed stare. A bloody surgical mask flaps from his ear. I don't feel sorry for him: he looks well past 60, the generation that screwed the rest of us over in their relentless pursuit of profit, comfort, greed. Truthfully, people seemed like zombies even before the infection, zoning out on their phones, obsessed with getting richer faster while everything else burns. Not that I'm bitter or anything.

He watches me in the tattered remains of his midnight-blue suit and eyes the red car. He doesn't come any closer. No balloon on him, so he must be a smarter one. I shift casually, so he stays in my periphery.

Vicki pops out, fresh lip gloss over her chapped lips. It doesn't surprise me anymore what people still do during an apocalypse. Anything to keep sane. For Vicki it was make-up, for Madison it was podcasts. For me, it was coffee. Of the few possessions in my backpack, I had developed a strong attachment to my miniature glass French press, wrapped carefully in two old T-shirts. It reminded me of better days. Now I just need to find some decent beans.

"I'm starving," Vicki moans. "Like, literally. I might faint."

We both scrutinize the gas station. "Don't see anything to eat."

Vicki shakes her head and groans again. "Plus, a guy with a shotgun. Never a good equation. Can't risk it."

I look at the maroon hybrid parked at the pump in front of us. Could have food. Cash. Weapons. Vicki follows my gaze and nods in agreement. It's amazing how even in a span of two days you can get to know someone well enough that you don't have to talk to communicate. One of the few perks of being in constant life-or-death situations, I guess.

Madison is nearing and I can feel her laser focus as she assesses what we're up to and falls in next to Vicki.

The three of us flank the empty car. Unlocked.

Out of the corner of my eye, I see our suited friend move.

"Mine," the zombie stammers like he's just learning to talk. "Leave it alone."

A glimpse of metal flashes from his side.

"He's got a knife—" I start to warn but realize no one's nearby. I turn a fraction to see Vicki and Madison aren't there. They've split, I realize as I hear car doors slam. Something in my gut twists up but I can't let emotions distract me. The zombie's sweaty forehead shines as he swings his hunting knife. I dodge but clumsily, banging into the side of the hybrid. I hear a rev from Madison's car.

Them ditching me hurts worse than any blade. Should've known better.

The dude shrieks and makes a wide arc with the knife again. I stumble as I duck. I can't get up fast enough—or maybe I don't want to—when he swings a third time.

Right before Madison's car slams into him.

Relief surges through me as I watch his figure flail over itself with a thud. Another sensation hits me: kinship. It's something I haven't felt in a long time.

"You guys..." I start to say and get choked up as they climb out. They look at me—Madison with her tired and bloodshot but relieved glance, and Vicki through her clumsily applied eye make-up—and I see they both get it, see that the three of us are in it together, for a while at least.

The guy's not like us, so I shouldn't feel bad, but something in me twinges in regret as we approach his body. He's twitching like a fish out of water, gasping out something about his wife. I'm always surprised at how much blood there is.

We had to do it, I tell myself as the three of us kneel next to him, ignoring his gasping pants. We all have to do whatever it takes to survive.

His kind was actually a blessing during food shortages. A few of us had found out their brains have a lot of nutrients in this post-apocalyptical hellhole, so, if you're really hungry, you have some options instead of starving. Rather than being gross like you might expect, their meat is dense and oddly tastier than a rich chocolate. Once you have a bite it's hard to stop. Like trying-not-to-eat-a-fresh-bag-of-chips-when-you're-stoned-hard.

"Zombie...." He slurs the word at me before his sentence disintegrates into a gurgled moan. "You...zombies."

"You should talk!" Vicki shrieks through her cracked lips. "It's people like you who got us into this shit show. Corporate boomer assholes."

"You tell him, babe," Madison murmurs.

The three of us started splitting his head open, his skull like a hairy, oversized walnut between our vise-like hands.

It's been too long since we've eaten, I realize as I slurp a chunk of his coiled brain matter. It's like butter-battered 5-star-restaurant crabmeat, the taste sending orgasmic shivers along my back. I've forgotten how this started, who had survived the infection and who had turned.

Forgot who the real zombies were.

WHAT STORMS BRING

Rosie had a venerable collection of talismans for emergency readiness, the most impressive of which was her waterproof go knapsack. In the straining nylon, objects of survival interlocked like a box puzzle: a water bottle, batteries, socks, bar soap, toothpaste, two cans of navy beans with the easy lift-off top, candles and a lighter.

On her coffee table, a flashlight rose singular and stark, a miniature testament to her readiness, a silo of technological fortitude. She had been lucky to get it. Yesterday, under a sky bloated with the weight of the impending storm, she had fled from store to store ravished by panicked consumers, finally spotting a corner of a flashlight's plastic casing that had slipped behind a rack of sympathy cards at the pharmacy.

Schools, subways, and offices across the region had already shut down for the day, as the hurricane was predicted to turn inland and merge with a growing nor'easter into a superstorm. Headlines on news pages grew in monstrous red print:

"LANDFALL OF PERFECT STORM IMINENT"

"COASTAL AREAS SLAMMED WITH RECORD WAVES"

Rosie was about to click a link to "HEAVY WINDS TOPPLING TREES RESULT IN 2 DEATHS" when she heard a bang outside.

She hurried to her first-floor bedroom window. There wasn't anyone at the door, just a small Halloween decoration of a homemade cloth ghost flapping on a string. The upstairs tenants were out of town and had texted asking if she could please bring in their yard decorations before the storm. Rosie had gathered everything else, but when she got to the dirty fabric and cavernous eyes of the makeshift ghost, she decided she would say it blew away.

She picked up her flashlight and ran her finger over the button in the back, pressing it in and out to make sure it still worked. At another bang, she jumped.

Someone was knocking.

Neighbors? Or the police for evacuation?

She went to the building's foyer and pushed the front door open against the wind that felt like it wanted to rip the door right off its hinges.

On the doorstep, a man squinted at her. Next to him rested a laundry cart of garbage bags flecked with raindrops.

Rosie blinked at him. The wind whipped her hair, and she tried to hold it down with one hand as the other braced the door.

The wind also snatched the words off her tongue. She tried again.

"Can I help you?" she shouted.

His eyes, caught between folds of skin, cast blankly behind her. Ends of gray hair moved beneath a winter cap. His whole face was the mealy texture of unbaked clay.

"Español?" Rosie asked.

She might have passed him before but not realized it, outside by the bus stop, where she always kept her eyes averted and clutched her purse as folks shuffled around, asking for change or muttering to themselves.

"Shouldn't you be in a shelter?" she said and thought of the headline HEAVY WINDS. "I don't know where one is, but I can look online—"

A gust of wind roared and his cap blew off, sending the gray strands dancing manically. His cart squeaked in protest and they both watched it clatter down the sloped street and out of slight. He turned unfocused eyes to her, opened his mouth, and closed it again.

She'd have to invite him in, she realized with a sinking feeling. After all, she was a Good Samaritan, she couldn't let him stay out here in the worst storm in recent history. She looked down the street at the rows of faceless townhouses and felt like they were the only two people for blocks. A few drops of rain fell on her bare arms.

He could stay in the basement, she thought suddenly. She wouldn't have to invite him into her apartment, and she wouldn't feel guilty either for abandoning him to the storm.

"You can wait it out downstairs," she shouted, gesturing with her free hand and stepping back.

Once the door was closed, she smoothed back her hair and looked at him again. He was so pale, as if his skin had never seen the light of day, except for mottled marks across his cheeks that reminded her of fruit beginning to over-ripen. His bony hands gripped a tired gray knapsack.

He didn't seem dangerous—though she knew better than to let her guard down around a stranger. A smell emanated off him, pungent and unwashed, and she tried to hold her breath.

He followed her down the unfinished, paint-splattered wood staircase to the basement.

"There's a small bathroom there if you need it." She breathed shallowly through her mouth to avoid smelling anything and used her no-nonsense work voice. "I don't think we'll get flooding since we're on a hill but if so let me know, OK? OK."

He slumped against the wall between her storage closet and the dryer and closed his eyes.

This is fine, Rosie thought. He could take a nap there until the storm passed.

Back in the living room, she stopped dead in her tracks. She bent under the coffee table, lifted the couch cushions, checked the kitchen. After a few minutes of searching she gave up, collapsing onto the couch in a fit of frustration.

Her flashlight was gone.

An hour had passed since she had let the homeless man in. Rosie had placed electronic tea lights around the coffee table as a replacement for her flashlight, and the rain had turned from a slow tapping to something more furious.

She peered out her bedroom window again to see a strange purple hue to the sky. The wind made a low, persistent whine. She closed her lace curtains, the fabric catching and soothing her eye. She had always loved miniature patterns: the entwining leaf motif on her tablecloth, plates with delicate floral borders, the hand-painted details on the Russian nesting doll collection smiling from the shelf in her hallway.

As Rosie walked back into her living room, she heard a hum. She cracked her apartment door and listened,

The washer? She ventured down the basement steps.

The man had cleaned up, stripped down to fuzzy long johns and a long sleeve shirt that hung in sags. Crumbled paper towels lay like flowers around him. Some color had moved back into his face. He hummed to himself, sitting straight against the wall and going through his gray knapsack with a particular fervor.

She cleared her throat, feeling awkward. She thought she ought to say something but didn't know what until it came out of her mouth. "I'll bring you something to eat."

He continued to hum something familiar as he took out items from his knapsack—a folded piece of ragged, once-white notebook paper, a letter opener, empty cereal bar wrappers, and other useless things—and stuffed them into the small trashcan that sat by the washer. He didn't look at her. She skulked back upstairs and into her apartment.

In one kitchen cupboard sat a small army of jugs of water. She couldn't spare a whole gallon—water was the most important thing in a disaster, after all—but she could bring him down a cup from the tap. Above the sink, stacks of alphabetized-by-brand cans of soup, vegetables and beans stood by to deliver their reassuring, heavily preserved nutrients. The bathtub and every large pot were full of water. She would be fine through the storm. She was utterly, completely prepared.

On the staircase, she left the water and a box of whole wheat crackers on the last step before darting back into her apartment.

She cracked her bedroom window open for a second. The trees and power lines swayed. She watched for a few minutes, waiting to see if anything would fall. The invisible eddies and crisscrossing of wind spun, knitting themselves up to a frenzy and she pictured herself being plucked right up, sent sailing along the currents until she was swept out into the dark sea beyond the harbor.

She closed the window.

In her living room, Rosie watched a New York woman with unpolished crystal chunks hanging from her neck tell an aghast reporter that she was going out into the storm to connect with Mother Nature. The news segment flashed to an older man in New Jersey wielding a metal detector and talking enthusiastically of the washed-up treasures he'd find during the storm.

When Rosie went downstairs again, the man was looking through her storage closet. He moved quickly, rummaging through her bins, the bare bulb from her open closet casting a blade of light across his hands.

"Um," she said. She didn't want to aggravate him in case he became angry or violent, but began contemplating the sensibility of calling the police when she saw he had put two books to the side. *He's just looking for something to do,* she thought. And she couldn't really blame him for wanting to read.

Rosie was about to turn to leave but did a double take, staring at the bins. She could have sworn hers were blue, but these were brown. She blinked and moved closer to touch them. It must have been the light, maybe warped by the hurricane somehow.

Next to the bins, a face on the cover of one of the books seemed to fix on her with a manic grin.

The paint speckles on the wooden stairs shifted as she walked slowly up. *There's something wrong with my eyes,* she thought.

The man hadn't looked at her once.

The storm screamed through the streets. The windows creaked and the lights flickered once, twice, but held. Online, photos and short articles were streaming faster than she could keep up. "WIDESPREAD DAMAGE" "TREE CRUSHES FAMILY" "DOG WALKER ELECTROCUTED" "THOUSANDS ALONG COAST WITHOUT POWER"

Rosie stared at a photo of a shark swimming next to a flooded suburban house's porch. For some reason, the photo deeply unsettled her, the black smear beneath the water, the shadow of a fin. *A fake*, she decided.

A sudden, hard rap sounded at the door. She thought of the ghost decoration and shuddered.

Ignore it, she thought. Nothing good came of her opening the front door today. She unplugged her phone, turning it in her hands. She had called her family that morning, telling them not to worry if they didn't hear from her since the power would probably go. But they were the anxious type, and surely they would have called by now to check on her?

Her phone was silent even though three bars of reception held steady.

On her computer streamed photos of water gushing into subway stops, houses with the facades torn off and cars floating down the street. The storm was still gathering power, moving north toward her.

Nothing is really ours, she thought.

Clatter, clatter. Like someone throwing metal trashcan lids at the front door, again and again. She clapped her hands to her ears and decided to venture downstairs again.

Her guest had pulled out a neon green lawn chair from her storage unit and was leaning back, munching on the crackers and flipping through an old Sherlock Holmes book. Two candles burned on ceramic holders on top of a boom box by his feet. The empty gray knapsack lay like a discarded skin on the top of the trashcan.

He looked more clean-cut, his hair shorn from some scissors he must have found in the basement. She touched her own hair, which felt heavy and greasy and gnarled.

She opened her mouth, but he hummed so she stopped. She

thought she might say "You must leave immediately" or even "Get the hell out," though she rarely cursed. But the words retracted and shrank, tumbling back down her throat.

She stumbled upstairs. The noise was louder at the door—*clatter, clatter, clatter.*

Her phone was missing. She threw the cushions from the couch, pushed the coffee table out of the way, and found it on the floor, its face blank. She snatched it up, plugged it in and jabbed the power button. Nothing. She popped the battery in and out.

CLATTER

"*Work*, you stupid thing," she said, jabbing the power button. She tossed it to the couch and went online to email her parents, but the browsers weren't responding.

"The mind can only handle so much change," she said aloud, staring at the blank screen. It sounded like a very logical statement.

She would put out her work outfit for the next day, as she always did. She always wore pants, never a skirt or dress, never jewelry that was too flashy. The storm would pass, and she would listen to her coworkers exchange stories of who had lost power, who had dealt with flooding.

It seemed like she had less to choose from than before. She took a blazer and set of pants out of the closet, both far too large for her. She examined a blue crisp men's shirt on a heavy black hanger.

"From the old tenant, of course," she said. Somehow, the previous tenant must have had left clothes in the closet, which she had missed when she moved in. "How irresponsible of them," she murmured.

Rosie sunk to the wooden floor, which was covered by a new red carpet. Her landlord must have placed it there without her noticing.

Just then, the power went out.

She grabbed an electronic tea light and went to look out the window through the curtains.

The streetlamp flickered over the rapidly flooding street. The ghost decoration twirled like a frenzied dancer between streams of rain before it tore off and raced into the darkness.

She started to pull the curtains closed and froze. The fabric—it had bold, dark splotches across it.

She brought the tea light closer. Those were definitely big, stark strokes of color, something she would never choose.

"I'm in the wrong apartment," she said. Shapes moved around her, and she stepped back from the decidedly not-lace curtains.

It's him, she thought. *He poisoned me somehow, he's making me hallucinate.* An aerosol attack. A reality TV prank.

She moved into the kitchen, picking up objects she no longer recognized: a swirled wooden bowl, a ceramic dog. Records? She didn't even have a record-player. Her coffee maker, her ice cream machine were both missing. Her hand groped in the dark empty space above the kitchen counter, faster and faster, knocking over jars and bottles of things she couldn't identify.

She threw the unmarked, unnamed jars to the floor, listening to the glass tinkle. She had to find a phone, call her family or friends but she couldn't remember anyone's name. Her mind went as blank as her phone screen when she tried to think of one.

"Surely I must know my own mother's name," she said to herself.

Dreading it, she reached up to the shelf that housed her beloved Russian doll collection. Her fingers brushed empty wall and the paper edges of a calendar.

She slid to the ground and sobbed just once, loudly. The wind was like a train tunneling into all the windows at once and she rubbed her ears. She heard the tree trunks in the back yard groan, as if they were pressing into the wall, about to crush her.

Still, she heard the clattering at the door, like someone hurling iron pots. "*What is that sound?*" she screamed and caught her breath.

She tore into the hallway, her gasp catching in her throat like a swollen mass of cotton. She would shove the man, punch him if she had to so he'd say something, so he'd look at her.

"What have you done?" she squeaked. The darkness swallowed her voice, and the wood and brick moaned under the weight of water and air. She felt her way down the stairs to the basement.

But he wasn't there. He was a step ahead of her. She had been readying herself for the wrong thing.

CLATTER CLATTER CLATTER

She stumbled on the last step but caught herself. The clattering at the front door was so loud she wanted to scream again.

That hum, that inane hum. What was that song?

She went back upstairs.

She had told herself she wouldn't open the door again, it seemed to only bring trouble. Yet the noise was too loud to ignore.

CLATTERCLATTERCLATTERCLATTER

She opened it, a flush of wind barging in and wrapping itself around her. His cart was there, pressed up against the door, stripped clear of its things except for a single translucent plastic grocery bag wound around one of the bars.

To the west the sky was a bruised darkness. The rain flung down, everything dripping and shimmering. A thin sheen of water lapped at the sidewalk, sloshing over from the street.

Next to her, APT 1 was missing her carefully printed last name. Instead, a handwritten "DANIEL C. CLARKE" was crookedly pasted there.

She reeled. A dream, surely.

She wrapped her fingers around the cart handle, pushing it away from the door to the sidewalk. Water soaked into her slippers and the rain beat her skin.

When she turned back, he was standing there, blocking the doorway, shiny new glasses reflecting blurry orbs of the streetlight and masking his expression.

Daniel put something down and nudged it toward her with a dark shoe. Her go bag.

The woman thought of the cans of soups and vegetables and jugs of water and was going to ask if she could have them as well, but for the first time Daniel seemed to look at her sternly, and she bowed her head.

"It's my apartment," she whimpered, but the wind ripped into her mouth and tore the words away into the silent open. She was about to try again to speak but felt the wind waiting, ready to pounce.

From one of his casual fingers, as though it had always been there, hung a keychain with door keys, car keys, laminated membership cards. Behind him, a dog barked a warning.

She felt a pinprick of tears but reached out to take the blue bag anyway. As soon as her fingers brushed the nylon, she felt the ties severe completely. Neighbors, family, work, all of it, gone, in one gasping breath. She was slipstreaming, caught somewhere that didn't matter while he belonged here now. She could only sense one tether: the winds snaking around her.

The full moon broke through the murky tendrils of clouds, and she could *see* the tether for a moment, stretching from above to tighten around her until she could displace it onto someone else, in another storm. She hummed a little to herself, feeling the vibration of her voice against her throat. The winds would allow that.

The woman was prepared a little, at least. She lifted the reassuring weight of her go bag into the cart, the bag that held her batteries, her soap and plastic bags, her notebook.

The wind tugged her cart in the direction of the receding storm. She took a step.

The front door slammed behind her.

THE COLOR OF FRIENDSHIP

THE CABIN, an edifice of glass panels and wood, pressed in by billows of clouds, emerged as the jeep jolted up the last of the switchbacks.

"Ladies' getaway weekend, here we come!" Brianna squealed and strained in the passenger seat to glimpse the lake. She started when she saw it; murky and dark green beneath the clouds, it made her think of sewage water. Certainly not the pristine blue in the rental pictures.

Just the lighting, she thought.

"Made it in time before the rain," Monique said, maneuvering the car up the muddy path.

"Thank God we have Wi-Fi." Ginger tapped at her phone.

Brianna resisted rolling her eyes. Of all the friends in their group, Ginger was the one she had hoped wouldn't be able to make their weekend getaway. She threatened to spoil everything with her snappy attitude. *Gingersnappy,* she thought, her private nickname for Ginger.

"It's so nice to take a break." Amita pressed her tablet off. "Remember the time, oh so long ago, before we had kids and jobs and responsibilities?"

"I can't believe it's been literally years since we've done a lake house cabin. Almost half a decade." Brianna smiled at memories of their high school New England weekend trips. She wiggled in her seat as they pulled to a stop in front of the door.

"So much glass, really?" Ginger's berry-glossed lips pushed into a frown. "Ugh, no privacy."

Brianna bristled, tugging on one of her curls. She was the one who had pored over dozens and dozens of Airbnbs, looking for the perfect listing. "I'm pretty sure I highlighted in the email thread the note about the glass. Sunlight reflects against the windows during the day and at night you just keep the lights dim."

"Not like there's anyone around to see us for miles," Monique said, turning off the car and stretching her perfectly manicured hands.

Brianna ignored a pang of jealousy and hid her own bitten, teal-colored nails in her fists. Monique was always polished but not overdone, and her French and South African accent and world-traveler vibe gave her a coolness Brianna couldn't even come close to.

They climbed out and unloaded their bags—Monique a slim duffel, Ginger a suitcase that looked more fitting for a week than a weekend, and Amita and Brianna with luggage somewhere in between.

Brianna grabbed two of the grocery bags with her free hand. "Steaks for tomorrow. Got Monique's favorite chips, gluten-free pastries for Amita, and tea for Ginger," she said and beamed at Amita's squeal of delight.

"You're like our personal assistant," Monique laughed. She said things like that sometimes and Brianna made sure to laugh too, even though the comment evoked pricks of irritation.

"The air is...weird. Is that the lake?" Ginger said. "Gag me."

"Smells like sewage." Amita wrinkled her nose and turned to Brianna. "Did anyone mention this in the reviews, Bri?"

Like she was supposed to read all of the hundreds of reviews. Even though she was the only one of them who was without a job—*between* jobs—it's not like she had all the time in the world.

"Hundreds of five stars." Brianna sniffed, trying to squash out any notes of defensiveness.

"Maybe something kicked up from the last few storms," Monique said. "Reminds me of being in NOLA."

Brianna punched the number in the keypad, and they fanned out into the living room. Inside the smell was gone, she noticed with relief, and everyone but Ginger oohed and aahed over the chic, modern rustic décor and the expansive fireplace. Brianna took on the role of hostess and pointed out the different amenities she had read about: Nespresso machine, hot tub, game room, and of course, lakeside access from the back. She demurred on the best room overlooking the lake, but the others politely insisted. Ginger's loud Facetime call with her supposed prodigy toddler floated through the house along with the hum of the TV as everyone settled in. Brianna lingered in her room, taking longer than needed to unpack as she admired the view.

Even though the color of the lake was still muted—gray green rather than azure—the water stretched larger and more majestic than the photos she had stared at for weeks in anticipation of this trip. A single bird's silhouette cut through the rolling fog over the water in the last of the twilight.

"I really needed this trip," Brianna declared aloud, but the others didn't chime in with their usual affirmations, probably unable to hear her over the TV and Ginger's blathering toddler. She half-listened for a mention of her name—someone admiring her work in finding this place or commenting on how much more together she looked than the last time they met at Amita's twins' baptism last year, when Brianna had arrived a smidge too tipsy.

"Heading to bed, night y'all!" Amita called, breaking Brianna's train of thought.

"See you in the morning for the hike," Brianna called back. "Rain should stop around 4am so hopefully it works out. Good night!" The others mimicked some version of the same.

Brianna dozed for a few hours before the sound of rain woke her up. Drops beat against the sliding glass door in her room so loud she thought someone was throwing rocks. She turned on the balcony light and cracked the door to see, beyond the stairs leading down to the lake, rain chopping the water, turning it into a black froth. Clouds ran like liquid illuminated by flashes of lightning. The entire room was glass, she reminded herself, but the idea of someone watching her, unlikely a possibility as that was, didn't scare her. Instead, curiosity—and a bit of excitement—nipped at her.

Until the stench of something rotten hit her nose, stronger than before, bordering on putrid. Her stomach twisted and she tried not to gag. Something the rain had kicked up, undoubtedly, and she wished it away.

"You aren't going to mess up this vacation," Brianna said to the smell and flipped off the light switch. The darkness pooled back onto the balcony.

The morning greeted them, clear and cool, as they hiked the five miles around the lake. It was like old times, Brianna thought triumphantly, brushing past the thick leaves and wiping the sweat from her forehead. Everything went just as she pictured, the rain holding off and the peacefulness ushered in a quiet, seeming to still the birds and insects into silence. Even Ginger seemed awed into being less annoying.

Brianna turned to Amita. "This is fun, isn't it?"

"It's so nice to get away." Amita brushed her short bob back and though her words were kind, Brianna felt a stab of some old pain leftover from when they were in high school, and Amita hadn't been as nice as she was now.

"I really needed this too. You know, I've been trying to figure out the next step in life." Brianna sidestepped a mud puddle surrounded by moss. "I kind of forgot how much I like to organize and lead. Maybe I need to find some way to channel that, you know, like an event planner business."

"What is *that*?" Monique's voice rang out.

At the edge of the lake, under long stalks the color of bile, sat a bundle of something on a patch of clovers. It looked like an army jacket, but as they neared the object, the septic-tank stench almost knocked Brianna over.

It wasn't a jacket, but leaves, tangled in clumps of mud. Flies swarmed above it.

"Is that seaweed?" Brianna gasped.

"Ratched." Ginger placed two fingertips on her nose. "I'm going to hurl."

Monique used a twig to poke at it. A nearly translucent paper-like chunk twisted up in the mud and leaves.

"It looks like snakeskin. Are there anacondas here?" Amita said.

"*Anacondas?*" Ginger said. Brianna took a discrete step back from the edge of the lake, so that Ginger was closest, just in case.

"Not this far north. That would be cool though." Monique chuckled. "It's probably just over-flooded systems, backing everything up."

"Sick," Ginger shuddered.

By the time they got back, the others decided to head in for a nap despite Brianna gently pressing them to try out the canoe, a banged-up thing the color of an olive left out too long.

No problem. She'd go out on her own. She untied the rope from the house's dock, determined to make the most of every minute of this trip. She glanced back to see the three of them in the kitchen, cutting limes for margaritas and laughing at something. A whisper of old pain hummed through her.

Not that she wasn't happy for her friends, of course she was. She was just catching up to them, on the brink of having it all together, like they did. She had, after all, been the one with the best grades, all the extracurricular activities, and Bobby as her boyfriend their junior year. But it fell apart when they were seniors. When Bobby broke up with her to go out with Amita, she had taken it in stride. And when Monique made valedictorian over her, *obviously*, Brianna was happy for her friend. And Ginger had gotten the fashion internship they had both tried for their first year of college. Monique was the smart one, Ginger ambitious, Amita prettiest. And where did Brianna fit in, aside from organizing their occasional get-together? Spinning her wheels, constantly waiting for the next big thing.

She stopped paddling to open a pistachio nut bar, forcing herself to—what did her therapist call it—*take a positive reframe*. Maybe this trip would be just what she needed to get her out of her rut, inspire her to find the precise course of actions to get her life back on track.

A gulp of water bubbled up next to her. Brianna screeched, dropping her bar into the lake.

A mound the size of a soccer ball and the color of overcooked peas broke the surface. A flipper—no, a hand. A cross between the two, with three dark green, finger-like webbed digits grasping the bobbing bar.

The flipper hand and bar disappeared.

A scream choked in Brianna's throat.

Don't call attention to yourself.

She forced herself to pick up the paddle but froze. *Alligator.* Brianna's thoughts struggled to name it. *Shark, fish.*

None of those.

Of course, it hadn't been a hand.

Some sort of lizard, obviously. She had dated someone with a pet iguana once. They could make good companions. Curiosity got the better of her and her breath came easier as the lake stayed still, peaceful. She lowered the paddle and rummaged in her backpack. She pulled out another bar, unwrapped it and threw a piece in the water, farther away from the boat.

After a second, bubbles appeared again, and the hand-flipper grabbed the bar. She waited, hoping to see more of the animal, but the water grew still again.

Brianna laughed to herself. "I made a friend."

Slowly, she paddled back, scanning the water for a sign, but the lake had closed up again. Her reflection moved along the glass of the cabin as she neared the dock, the boat cutting a symmetrical scar through the swampy water. She tied up the canoe and hurried up the porch stairs to tell the others.

"She can't even get her life together after what, decades?" Ginger's voice was low through the screen door. "Laid off, drinking *so* much. That girl needs to look in the mirror, but she's allergic to the truth."

Brianna froze. *Just go in,* she told herself. Surely, they weren't talking about her.

"She does seem to be struggling," Amita admitted.

"You can't say anything." Monique paused for a second. "But before the drive, she told me she's probably getting a divorce. So if she's kind of off, I bet that's why."

The air disappeared from Brianna's chest while the ground reeled. *Stop,* she wanted to yell but couldn't move.

"Maybe that's why she's so desperate. So *passive aggressive*. How many times did I try to bail, and she changed the reservation to make it work?" A jangle of Ginger's charm bracelet before she continued. "And she's like, literally green with envy when we talk about *anything*. Someone should do her a favor, tell her straight up to move on. This is my last pity trip. I wouldn't have come at all if it weren't for you guys."

"It's kind of nice having her around," Monique said. "And we're her friends."

"Are we though?" Amita said, hesitant. "I mean, we hardly talk..."

Brianna bit her lip to keep from sobbing as she backed away from the door. She grabbed a bag of chips that had been left in the car and headed to the lake loop by herself.

Passive-aggressive.

Brianna had run the accusation over in her mind a thousand times by the time she was a mile out. How could Ginger say that about her? And the rest agree?

Memories drifted to her as she rubbed tears away. They couldn't have known how, when she found out about Bobby, she had snuck into Amita's house to let her cat out, never to be found again. Or how, when Ginger got valediction, she had keyed her car. She had been careful, meticulous. She had needed to do those things to forgive them, ultimately. Childish, she knew. She wasn't perfect, but she was trying.

She threw some chips on the water and held her breath hoping— she didn't know what for. It was stupid, but her breath seemed to come easier when she saw the bubbles appear on the surface. It wasn't a hand this time, but a set of protruding eyes, ringed with emerald bands.

Watching.

The head rose from the water and paused. Almost adult-human sized, but gray, with a ridge along its top that rippled in the breeze. An oblong, lipless mouth puckered between rows of gills.

In the back of her mind, thoughts sprang up simultaneously,

running in a loop of their own accord, while the rest of her body crashed and short-circuited, torn between screaming and running.

This must be a new species of creature, she should call someone, maybe it was dangerous, maybe she'd get her picture in the paper, mutated, genes, undiscovered—

She took a step back, sucking in a breath to scream. The creature cocked its head, reminding her of a Labrador she once had. She noticed its mouth again—opening and closing.

"Are you...hungry?" she asked.

It opened its mouth again.

She tossed the full bag of chips. Its finned hand scooped up the snack into its mouth. At least she could do something right. Its round shoulders rose from the water, covered in barnacles. A smell, like a public toilet had exploded, hit her. Her stomach lurched but she ignored it, too fascinated by how the creature ate. Rows and rows of tiny fangs flashed in the receding light like a rusty zipper. Its tongue, the color of smoked salmon, flicked out to catch crumbs.

"Where did you come from? You look as lonely as I feel," she told it, dabbing at her wet eyelashes. It felt good to talk to something, someone, even if it was a lizard creature. "Real friends help each other, you know? They don't stab you in the back."

It slowly blinked its jewel-like eyes and slipped under the water. She stayed for a while, waiting to see if it would come back up.

When the sun had set, she finished the loop, but her thoughts kept churning like broken glass in a blender. By the time she came back in, Amita was standing alone, scrutinizing the inside of the fridge, empty solo cups, dirty plates, and a chip bowl on the counter behind her.

Amita turned. "We thought you fell in."

"You're supposed to be my best friends," Brianna managed, hating how she sounded like she was in high school all over again. Desperate. Lonely. And worst of all, whiny. "I heard you. Earlier."

Amita's forehead creased into the lines it did before she laughed or cried. "Listen, we are your friends. But we're not in high school anymore."

"What does that mean?" Brianna wouldn't let her look away. "Just tell me."

Amita sighed. "You wanted to be liked to the point of obsession. You still do, and it's hurting you. Look, I'm only telling you because I'm your friend."

"Friend." Brianna repeated. *Practice radical honesty,* her therapist had urged her, and Brianna squeezed the words out now. "Sometimes I feel like you guys don't appreciate me."

"That's exactly what I mean! Your obsession with validation seems...pathological. I know you're getting help, that's really good."

"Maybe if you hadn't betrayed me." It came out harsher than Brianna meant, and Amita gaped at her in surprise.

"Are you still sore about Bobby? Wow. Um, that was decades ago, Bri."

"I know that. I'm just saying it threw me off." Her voice wavered. "Made me out of step with my life."

Amita shook her head, eyebrows raised. "Are you serious right now?"

"Never mind, that's not what I meant. I'm tired." Brianna pushed past her to take out her leftover grilled steak. "Whatever. See you in the morning."

Brianna went to her balcony and watched the moonlight rim the lake, sharper than a mirror shard. The inside of her eyes felt raw and scraped, everything in her empty. If only she could will herself to disappear.

Once the house was silent, she tossed the steak as far as she could toward the water.

"Hey friend," she said when the stench of sewage floated up. "At least we look out for each other."

The lake creature stood a few feet from the base of the balcony stairs, its jade-like eyes glowing. The ridge along its head stretched like a fan and Brianna caught her breath. The creature looked so strong, so *different*, it was almost beautiful under the moonlight. Beads of lake water rolled down the knotted muscles of its finned limbs. It stretched taller than her, with a short torso and long rubbery legs. Its teeth flashed as it tore into the steak. Half a layer of discarded scales clung to it, a smaller skin it had shed.

It swallowed the last bite and gnashed its teeth, watching her.

She left the sliding door open and stepped down from the balcony, keeping her distance. The lake creature opened its mouth again. Pleading, she realized, for her to help.

"You're still hungry, huh? Poor thing."

It cocked its head and the thought of someone that strong, that unusual, needing her help, made her brighten. It all clicked into place. She wasn't the one who needed to change, to disappear.

They were.

"Not friends." Brianna pointed toward the open door. She felt lighter than she had in a long time. Like she was finally on the right path. This is what her therapist might have meant by *standing up for herself*, by *cutting out toxic friendships*.

"Food. Go ahead."

The lake creature rushed forward and up the stairs into her bedroom, fast as an ape. She untied the boat and let it go silently out on the water by itself while shouts rose up behind her.

"Oh my God! Oh my God!" Ginger screamed.

Brianna looked back.

Through the glass walls of the cabin lit by a soft hallway nightlight, the lake creature clamped onto the back of Ginger's neck until the kitchen knife slid from her hand. Red bloomed down her shoulders. The creature charged down the hallway to lift the thrashing form of Amita over its head and twisted her like a rag doll until she was limp. It shot forward to grab Monique, who was trying to barricade herself into the bathroom, and slammed her against the wall. Catching all its food, Brianna realized, so it could eat slowly, in peace. It would feast well tonight.

At least Brianna had been a good friend to someone.

She'd clean up in a bit, take Monique's car, let authorities know they had taken a late-night drunken boat trip.

It was a boating accident. They disappeared in the water.

Resolution flowed into her as she gazed across the dark green water, still as a mirror under the moon. She'd find new friends. And if they took advantage of her too, well, she could always suggest a trip to the lake house.

LONELY ARCADE

THE BOARDWALK ARCADE, which stank like rotting driftwood, is where Trish first saw the ghost.

At first, she thought it was a dirty smudge on the wall in the corner arcade where no one went but her. During summer break, all the other 6th graders hung out at the glitzier game center a block down, but Trish preferred to weave through the small labyrinth of carnival-like stalls, dodging people clutching stuffed animals of questionable integrity. There, amidst the ancient consoles flashing lights in hopes of a player, she could be alone. She had beaten all the games except for one.

When she looked up again, the ghost appeared, the height of an 8-year-old. Sand-streaked hair with a sagging bow of seaweed. A fluffy white dress, that was more tears than fabric. The rest of her blurred in a way that was hard to see next to Mortal Kombat.

The ghost's mouth moved silently, a slash darker than the sea at night. She pointed at the floor and then the ceiling.

Trish snatched her coin cup and ran all the way back to the vacation rental several blocks away.

"It was a friggin' ghost." Trish lifted a hand to show her parents. "This tall. Standing right there."

Her mom's eyes narrowed, her irritation at Trish's antics eclipsing the pain that had settled there since the funeral. "You're spending too much time alone again. Go find some friends."

Trish wandered the boardwalk through the throng of burnt shoulders, scanning her phone for any accounts of ghost stories on the boardwalk, of tragedies. She bookmarked one story, about a foster girl who had hid on the boardwalk during a hurricane. Her body was never found.

"Sad," Trish said aloud, studying the black-and-white photo of wreckage from the boardwalk collapse.

Curiosity got the better of her, but the old arcade was silent except for the machines' beeps. After she checked every corner for shadows, she started to play. Her tokens dwindled in their plastic cup. When she looked up from the pixelated X-Men, the ghost was standing next to her, its eyes gleaming the palest blue, like a shell bleached too long in the sun. The girl's mouth gaped open like a fish.

"Are you ..." Trish tried to be brave. The mournful yearning in the ghost's eyes reminded her of her younger brother before he died, after his cells rebelled in destructive protest. "...sad?"

The ghost pointed at something on the floor. A long extension cable. Trish's eyes followed the ghost's gesture up toward the ceiling fan.

Trish bent down to grip the brown cable and shuddered, picturing a homemade noose. "What, you want me to join you?" One of the games blared to life next to her, as if someone was playing. Agreeing.

"I get it. We could play video games forever. Not be bothered by anyone."

It was tempting. To not have to face another school year, the pitying looks of her teachers, the whispers of her classmates. Her parents. They were so burdened already, maybe it would be easier for them if Trish wasn't around. They could have a fresh start.

A kid squealed outside, and Trish thought for a second it might be her brother, clutching one of the cheap stuffed lions from a boardwalk game she had won last year.

But he's gone.

She wiped the wetness from her cheeks.

"I get you're lonely," Trish whispered. "I am too. But I can't stay…" she gestured to the games. "*Here.* I have to move on."

The ghost watched her as she backed up and out of the dingy arcade. Outside, she sucked in a lungful of sea breeze threaded with vinegar and popcorn. She walked toward the new game center a block away, her step a little lighter.

THE SIGHTING

THE TEETH MARKS were like none Mae had ever seen.

"Finally." Mae kept calm though she wanted to shriek in excitement. She placed her ruler against the bark of the tree. Ralph pushed a branch out of the way to watch as she measured.

"Primate-like. And wider than human." Mae snapped photos and carefully scrapped out the bark around the bite mark. "Hopefully we can DNA sequence any trace of saliva. I can't believe it."

Mae had been fascinated in the creature—Bigfoot, Sasquatch, whatever you called it—for as long as she could remember. Once she started training as a dentist's assistant, she poured over Bigfoot forums and blogged her ideas. After scrutinizing photos people posted of unusual bite marks on bones, she became more convinced that the creature did, indeed, exist. She doubled down on her efforts at the cost of friends and dates. Even her parents were exasperated with her obsession.

"Why is it so important for you?" they'd plead. "What does it matter?"

"It *matters*," Mae had said. She couldn't explain it. Ever since she was a kid she had been ignored—for being too quiet, too odd, too smart. But now she knew she was destined for something more: to prove Bigfoot existed.

She had found Ralph through the forum, who offered tours to Bigfoot scholars around the national forest in Southern Oregon. She would have gone on her own but reports of missing people—some Bigfoot hunters that got hopelessly lost in the vast forest after wandering away from their guide—prompted her to take extra precautions. She wasn't going to make the same mistake.

When she had met Ralph at the visitor's center that afternoon, she quizzed him. He needed a shave beneath tired eyes, and his cargo pants could use an iron, but he was sharp with his responses.

"What does Bigfoot eat?" she asked.

"Simple question, not so simple an answer." He leaned against a wildlife display and chewed a strip of jerky he pulled from a cammo backpack. "Eyewitnesses suggest it isn't fast enough to catch a deer, or strong enough to wrestle a bear. But size-wise it would need a lot of food."

"That's right," she said. "Cryptozoologists believes Bigfoot hunts large game. Some think it's smart enough to trap animals, maybe small mammals. What about vegetarian?"

Ralph shook his head. "Accounts of bone stacking, droppings, and teeth marks suggests it really likes meat."

"Right—possibly a pure carnivore, unlike other apes and humans." Mae nodded, satisfied that he was sufficiently well versed and wasn't just looking to rip off a "believer" like other tour guides. She was also well aware she was a solo woman going to a campsite with a man she didn't know, but his extensive positive Yelp reviews—and the taser in her bag—reassured her.

"So why do you do it?" Mae had asked him as they climbed into his four-wheeler. "Most people say Bigfoot hunters like us are delusional." *Or worse*, she added silently, trying not to think of the sidelong glances or the muffled laughs she had gotten at school or at work when someone found her blog.

Ralph looked sheepish. "Honestly? The money's good, and I love these woods. But I'm also in awe of the passion this community has.

And…" He gave her a mischievous grin. "Think how famous I'll be when the first real evidence is found."

"How famous *we'll* be." She smiled back. *Don't get distracted,* she told herself. But it was rare to meet a guy who didn't completely write her off, who understood just what a big deal this could be.

His four-wheeler had jostled over rocks as they traveled north. She had been quiet, making a pact with herself. If she didn't find something this time, maybe it was a sign that she should give up the search for good. She couldn't spend her life chasing an invisible monster, after all. It was now or never. They parked, donned backpacks, and dove into the brilliant green to a spot she had traced as the epicenter of the last three sightings, finding the telltale marks on a tree a few hours later.

"It could be a wild boar," Ralph mused now, touching the teeth marks in the bark.

"Nope." Mae inhaled the scent of dirt and wet leaves, feeling more alive than she had felt in a long time. "This is almost a two-inch tooth impact mark. No other known animal could do this. Not quite what I need but close."

"What do you mean?" Ralph asked.

"It's all in the teeth. The back teeth to be exact. I believe Bigfoot has a distinct pattern of modified carnassial molars unlike any known primate—sharp back teeth, essentially, for tearing into flesh. If I can get some clear pictures of that, it would be evidence of its existence. And it would help us understand if it's a totally new kind of ape."

"Most people come in with vague ideas and have no idea how to track." Ralph looked more alert, excited even. "But you actually have a good theory there."

Mae tried not to blush as their eyes met. She couldn't remember the last time someone complimented her in real life. Ralph cleared his throat, ran a hand through his uncombed hair and glanced down at his watch.

"Getting dark," he said. "We should find a campsite soon. I'm starving. I'll scope for a spot while you finish looking around."

"Sounds good. Do you want to—" Mae gasped and leaned down to brush away leaves to reveal a flash of white.

A pile of bones, stacked in neat crisscrosses.

Large bones.

She dropped her bags. "Oh my God. I need to take some pictures. Do these look like deer bones?"

Ralph peered down in the dimming light. "Wider than deer, I'd say."

"Look at how they're stacked. There's real intention there." Mae blinked back tears. All that time alone, all the friends she hadn't made, all her countless hours looking...*finally* meant something.

"Any chance it could be a coincidence?" he asked.

"It's way too symmetrical. The stacking indicates a ritualistic observance, almost like a burial," she said as she steadied her trembling hands to take pictures. This, together with teeth marks and saliva samples and she'd have it: the world's first real evidence of Bigfoot. She'd give interviews, maybe even on live TV. Possibly a book deal. Funds and teams to continue to track and understand Bigfoot. She'd be the next Jane Goodall.

"This gives weight to the theory that Bigfoot is extremely intelligent, and potentially communicative," she continued, hushed. "Ralph, I think we're close. Like, actually close. We have to keep going."

A branch snapped and she looked up to see Ralph, looming and shaggy in the snatches of light, his figure seeming taller by the second. "You're definitely on its trail. But let's eat first," he said and yawned.

That's when she saw his teeth.

THE U TRAIN

THEY SAY WAITING IS its own kind of hell. Whoever said that was probably familiar with the NYC subway system.

"Think it's the End of Days?" A gentleman to my left asked. We both stood at the edge of the yellow strip on the platform, waiting for the train. God knows how much time had passed. Over an hour at least. I had gotten up early to go to my favorite breakfast spot in East Harlem. Bacon to die for. My doc said I shouldn't eat so much bacon. Or smoke. Or drink soda. But don't they all say that?

"It's always the End of Days waiting for the transfer," I responded, and he chuckled. He jiggled his foot and was going to ask me something else, but I turned my attention pointedly away. Even though he was well dressed—collared shirt and a suit jacket visible from his open windbreaker—you could never tell who would ask for money or start talking crazy at you. I took stock, automatically, at how many people were around us. Just two others this early, a guy maybe in his early twenties with a faded rainbow hoodie and oversized headphones, and a woman around the same age, shrugging off a purple peacoat as she balanced a covered tray of cupcakes.

"I hate to ask but do you have a portable charger I could borrow? My phone is dead." The suited man said. As evidence he opened his hand, where the screen of his new smart phone-what-not was blank as a slate.

I shook my head. "Never had a need. Don't want anyone tracking me. You know they can hear everything you say on those. I got nothing to hide, but my business is also my business."

He cocked his head, puzzled like just about anyone who learned I didn't have a phone, his foot pausing for two seconds before resuming its tapping. "It's just...I'm not sure why the U train is so late. And *I'm* going to be late."

He gestured up and I followed his line of thought. It was an older station and hadn't been fitted with any of those automated screens hanging overhead or announcers that told you how long it'd be. No attendants either; I'd have to track back up a long set of stairs and a godforsaken endless corridor to find a living person back at the turnstiles.

"Just like back in the day," I grunted. "You had nothing to tell you how long it'd be, half the time. Transfers, busses, constructions. People throwing themselves on the tracks. Happens a lot, you know. You just have to wait."

"Have you heard an announcement?" The girl chimed in behind us, setting the cupcakes on the rusted steel bench.

"Check your phone?" Suit asked.

Cupcakes shook her head, pressing a stray blond strand behind her ear. Genevieve would be about her age now, but I didn't want to think about that. "It's not turning on."

Suit held very still. "Mine either. Which is weird, I always charge it."

Both considered a moment before Cupcakes tapped the guy with headphones. His shoulders tensed and he turned.

"Do you know if the train's late?" Cupcakes loudly and pointed to his faded jean pocket, where a sliver of a phone stuck out. "Could you check? Please?"

Headphones shrugged. "Outta juice."

"So what are you listening to?" Cupcakes said.

He slid his headphones down and around his neck. "People don't bother me as much when I wear them," he said, almost defensive.

"Something's not right," Suit said. "How can all of our phones not be working?"

"That's why I don't carry the things," I said. "Look how distraught you all are over a piece of plastic and metal. Cyberattack, cancer in the brain. No thank you."

I glanced at my watch but had forgotten to wear it this morning. Damn. My wrist felt bare as a newborn's butt. The line out of my breakfast place would be unacceptable by 8:30, 9 tops. Then I'd be late for chess in the park. If I was a minute past the hour, Pete would mosey in on my prime corner seat like it hadn't been my spot the last ten years. I'd have to wait a half hour at least for rounds, then late to lunch.

"Damn it," I growled. "I need my coffee."

"You gonna look for a transfer?" Cupcakes asked, glancing behind her. I followed her gaze.

The exit seemed miles away. I'd have to zigzag up and down countless steps, trek up intersecting corridors, sidestepping pedestrians. In the meantime, I'd get breathless and covered in sweat that would turn cold and sticky against my sweater and make me uncomfortable all day. And as subway luck would have it, the train would probably roll up as soon as I left.

"Nah," I said. I looked out on the tracks to entertain myself, see if I could spot something, anything. Maybe a rat to flick a rubber band at. If there was one thing I hated it was rats, so any chance to kill 'em or cause them a little suffering was time well spent. But not a soul moved down there. I strained my ears, listening for the faint drone or screech of an approaching subway. Nothing. Just the tap-tap-tap of Suit's foot, Cupcake's sighs, and somewhere down that dark tunnel, a steady drip. The usual subway smell—a baked-in stench of old garbage, fresh pee and smoke topped with a sprinkling of fungus or mold—flared in my nose.

"What's that?" Headphones asked.

"Dessert, for a going-away party," Cupcakes answered. She wasn't dressed right for the weather or the morning, in some sort of sequined flare skirt and halter top. Not that I didn't appreciate the look, mind you, but April was full of endless wet and slush with a few teasing peekaboos of warm weather, so tantalizing you wanted to scream.

"At this hour?" I gave her a look. I mean, really peered over my glasses at her. *Who the hell has a party at 7am?* I wanted to ask and looked at my wrist again, forgetting the watch wasn't there.

Cupcakes sniffed and shifted, avoiding my eyes. Probably guessed me to be a lecherous old man. I didn't want to break it to her, but she wasn't my type at all, too skinny. Something in my DNA just didn't find that all that interesting.

"Dead as a doornail," Suit said again in frustration, jabbing at his phone. "I don't hear anything. You think maybe something happened?"

Headphones' eyes lit up. "Like a Godzilla type? Or a terrorist attack?"

"I think we'd hear screams," Cupcakes said.

Headphones shrugged and headed toward the stairs without another word. We watched his backpack move up and out of sight.

"I'm too old for this sh—" I started when Headphones popped back down.

"What's the word?" Suit said.

Headphones blinked at us. "I went up and…. I'm back."

I squinted at him. "What are you going on about?"

"I can't leave," he said. "I can't. Like physically can't."

Suit jogged up the staircase and, a second later, jogged right back down. He paused on the last step, looking at us, up, down, up again like he was watching an invisible tennis match. Then his face folded like so many cards.

"It's not real. It's not right," Suit moaned.

Headphones had buried his face in his hands. "Wake up. Wake up."

"You guys are as hilarious as a battle sub with a screen door." I glanced behind me just to make sure there were no cameras. "This one of those viral marketing stunt flash mob what-have-yous? Hilarious."

I snorted and heaved myself up the stairs. When I got to the top, I found myself facing downwards, looking at the platform again. I turned to go back up and was facing down again. The whole effect made me dizzy, so I shuffled down the last few steps and onto the bench next to Cupcakes.

"You try," I croaked at her, and she shook her head, eyes wide and terrified as a mouse.

"Screw this!" Suit bellowed at the empty track. "I'll go down there and walk to the next access point if I have to."

He stood, half crouched as if to jump down. He glanced at the rest of us and wavered.

"Sit down amigo." I laughed to hide my nerves. "You're not going anywhere. Whatever thing is happening *up there* is trying to keep us *down here*. You think they haven't thought of that?"

Headphones finally lifted his head as Suit arched an eyebrow. "*They?*"

"Government corporate types, who else? We're just pawns on their board. If there's an outbreak, or a terrorist attack, or what have you, you think they don't have sophisticated weapons? They got all kinds of things. Including—" I waved my hands toward the stairs. "Invisible force fields, walls, what not."

"Sounds like conspiracy crap," Suit said.

"Believe it or not but it's well documented. It was always a matter of time. You'll see."

Trick was you had to look for the little offbeat blogs and forums, the ones where people talked in code and told you what was really going on behind the curtain. I knew some of it was hogwash, sure, but when you lived as long as I had, you know sometimes there's kernels of truth in the unlikeliest of places.

"They don't want us out, we're not getting out," I tried to explain but they were all panicking. Headphones and Cupcakes shouted for help at the stairs until they were hoarse. Stupid kids. Suit did eventually climb down to the tracks and walk a few feet down in the darkness, just to turn around.

"Same as the stairs," Suit huffed as Headphones helped him back up on the platform. Suit shrugged off his windbreaker and hurled it against a post. "What the fuck are we supposed to do?" He slumped onto the bench next to me, defeated.

Something like a skittering sounded below the tracks. I glanced down, looking for the shiny brown back of a roach or tail of a rat.

"You hear that?" I asked.

"No, what?" Suit cocked his head and we all listened. Nothing.

"Maybe nothing." I shrugged. "Maybe a sewer rat or giant roach. Some of 'em grow to be the size of your whole arm, no kidding. Prehistoric."

"It's gotta be a dream." Suit pinched the back of his hand. We watched his skin turn white then red. "Ow."

"I think it's an end-of-the-world sitch," Cupcakes said, her dress spread out as she sat on the bench. "Actually, I'm relieved. It's about time."

The rest of us looked at her as a flush crept, relentless, along her cheeks. "I mean, I'm just tired of it all, you know?"

More silence until Headphones piped up. "Yeah."

"What, your expensive liberal arts college got you blue?" I asked.

"I have a lot to worry about actually." A mix of shame and pride stormed over her face, reminding me of a kid. "No, I, ah, dropped out of school. Run a pretty successful business selling stuff."

"Stuff?" I already knew where she was going by her tone, and I wasn't impressed. How does that song go, lots of "good girls gone bad" in the city.

She nodded curtly.

"Pot?" Suit said hopefully and she shook her head.

"You don't look anything like a dealer," Headphones said. She smiled primly but then I noticed the bags under her eyes, how her forearms looked like any fat or substance was burned right off, leaving the thinnest skin stretched over bones.

"That's what makes it so easy," she said and, almost as an afterthought, added, "it's a lot of money."

"Better be careful with that nonsense," I said. "People fall down a hole faster than they can get out."

She nodded, her eyes hollowed as a skeleton.

"Well, might as well make things interesting," Suit said. "I screwed my trainer yesterday. Again." He breathed out, bounced a bit on the balls of his loafers. "Man, it feels good to get that out. My wife ever found out well…" His glance flicked down for a second. "She's a little unstable. Makes it hard." He made a sound like a laugh, a noise mixed with heartbreak and relief. "She'd probably shoot me point blank."

"That's fucked." Cupcakes glanced at his wedding band.

"Pssh, you think that's a big dark secret?" I asked. "Show me a man in this world that hasn't cheated, once."

Headphones rose his hand.

Cupcakes rolled her eyes at me. "So what's your deal?"

"I'm not interested in games," I said and looked at the rail. I glanced at my bare wrist again out of habit and couldn't shake the urge of too much time passing. It must have been hours by this point. Probably almost lunch time.

"Guys." Headphones' hand was shaking.

"You OK, kid? Gonna barf?" I stepped back to be safe.

"I um, just remembered something." He was actually shaking, like he was cold, teeth chattering and everything. "There is no U subway."

Cupcakes started counting on her short purple nails. "F, L, 2. There are others, so many." She blinked. "Every day I take the…" She looked at us in confusion.

I wracked my brain but couldn't remember a damn thing about my commute.

"What does it mean?" Suit asked. "I can't…I can't even remember my name."

"Deadly toxin." I nodded. "Eating out our brains. Causing early onset dementia."

Cupcake yelped and covered her face. "Don't *say* that."

"I think—" Headphones shook his head, a grim set to his jaw. "We're in some kinda limbo. Maybe hell. I had a dream, last night." He pulled a beat-up blue spiral notebook the size of a checkbook from his back pocket. He flung it open and flipped past fraying corners to the last page. A sketch in pencil, not half bad, looked up at us, recognizable enough. The reaper.

"Now *that* is crazy," I said, angrier than I intended.

"Wait…" Suit said and leaned against the filthy column for support as his eyes fluttered closed. "Maybe it's true. The last thing I remember is...well, I can't recall, but I think it wasn't good. Maybe we're dead."

At his words something stirred in me, a panic, a quick realization that something was wrong, but I smothered it as quick as a bag of unwanted pups.

Headphones, however, nodded vigorously. "And now waiting for the ferry guy."

"Ferry guy?" Cupcakes squeaked. "You mean, like the River of the Dead? God that's morbid. How about an angel or something more positive?"

"Angels *down here?*" Headphones spread his hands.

"You won't entertain the likely notion that it's the government or terrorism but think we're all dead. That's rich." I laughed to cover up the lump that was forming at the base of my throat. Like I had swallowed something that the acid reflux wanted to send back up.

Cupcakes, Suit, and Headphones all seemed subdued, somber. Now that had me unraveling like my cheap sweater. The lump in my throat seemed to grow, dropping into my stomach heavy as a sack of nails. I tried not to think about all I hadn't done with my life yet despite my years, all the people I still had something to say to. I pushed the sensation away, but one thought burrowed under my skin and stuck. Pete in my seat, setting up the chessboard. Smug bastard would probably be glad I was dead.

Suit paced in short circles, the shadows on his face jumping in the gloom. "So what is this? Our last confessional?" He looked up at the dank, spotted ceiling and was really yelling now. "I didn't do anything to deserve this. So I cheated, so *what?* I didn't murder anyone. Didn't fuck up that bad. Not enough to be down here!"

Watching his breakdown made me feel a little better. Gave me some entertainment at least.

"Get a grip," Cupcakes said and turned to Headphones. "If it is a confessional, maybe you two need to go ahead with yours so we can wake up from this nightmare, move onto the next world or whatever."

"You seem awfully calm." Suit's note of accusation was sharp as a shard of whiskey bottle. "Are you the devil?"

"What? *No.*" Cupcakes flushed. "Now you sound like my ex."

"OK." Suit pointed to Headphones. "What's your deep dark secret then that earned you this hallowed place besides us, Adulteress and Drug Dealer?"

"Me?" Headphones looked embarrassed and fiddled with the bent spiral of his notebook. "I, ah, some of my friends beat up guys sometimes. Homeless dudes mostly. Some guys are into it. It's kinda funny. I can't explain it. They usually don't fight back. You kinda have to be there."

"O-M-G," Cupcakes said.

"I didn't do anything," Headphones said hastily. "Just watched. The cops came though and... I don't really remember, I was kinda outta it."

The other two looked disgusted and he hung his head. "I know. I'm a piece of shit."

All their faces turned toward me, curious, relentless. Screw that, I started to say but stopped. Something in each of them had opened up it seemed, with their confessional. Less hardened and evasive. Just sort of sad. Reminded me of the last time I saw my other little girl, Pipa. Somehow she knew I was planning to leave, even though I didn't give any hint. Didn't pack anything. Said I was going to work as usual, gonna be late.

"Few kids," I barked hoarsely. "Haven't seen 'em in a while."

That was all I had to say about that. But Cupcakes regarded me sadly, and she started to remind me of the kiddos I had upped and left.

"Cut that out, with the big eyes," I said, and she blinked. "I tried but it didn't work out."

Suit nodded vigorously. "There's something about being free, yeah?"

I didn't want to talk about it anymore. I went back to the yellow stripe and looked down. No trash on the tracks. That should've been my first sign that something was wrong.

"It's too late to do anything about it now," I said to the tracks.

Cupcakes sighed. "It's never too late."

"Sometimes it is, though," Headphones said.

"You hear that?" I strained my ears. Finally, what sounded like the faintest drone echoed somewhere down the tunnel.

Cupcakes' eyes grew enormous, and Suit's mouth was a perfect "o" that would've made me laugh under other circumstances.

"The train," Headphones said, unnecessarily.

I had never been religious but damn if it didn't say a quick prayer right then.

Dear Lord. Please please let this be all some sort of screwy dream and let me wake up. I'll be better I swear. I'll reach out to the kids—even though they'll tell me to shove it—I'll do it anyway. I swear. If you gimme a chance. Please.

The others were quiet, probably in their own negotiations.

I shuffled behind the yellow line as the train roared up and the doors to the last car screeched open. The cars in front of it were dark and closed.

"Could be a test." I still half suspected it was a government job. I glanced in. I expected ghouls or zombies or something, but it was empty, a little dirty.

"Typical car by the looks of it," I said.

"Should we board?" Headphones asked.

Suit pushed past me to step on. "*Anything's* better than here."

"Let's hope," Cupcakes murmured.

Headphones laughed nervously as we boarded. "We're good maybe."

Once we were all on the doors whooshed closed and the subway started, lights flickering. Nothing weird, nothing off, until Headphones stood at the window.

"We're definitely in Hell," Headphones said with a certainty that made us look over.

"How do you know?" I went to stand next to him as he pointed.

Through the rear window, below the track that we were zipping along, squirmed bodies. Hundreds, maybe thousands.

And not just any bodies.

The four of us. Over and over again. All squirming and mashed up on each other, grinning and waving in a mass of glittering skirts and suit jackets and rainbow hoodies and fraying Argyle sweaters, making up a fabric like a ribbon undercutting the city.

Cupcakes screamed and Headphones doubled up, dry heaving again.

I couldn't stop staring. We were moving too fast to really focus on a single face, but the quick flashes of my smug smile, gnarled hands flicking toward the sky, and shock of gray hair made me dizzy. It was like looking into a pit of cracked mirrors as the train thundered on, rolling over infinite versions of ourselves.

Cupcakes shuddered finally. "I can't look anymore. This is a bad trip. The worst."

"I think you're right, kiddo. We're in purgatory." Once I said it aloud, a little flint of a memory came back to me. Pain, and collapsing from my bed. Maybe I should've listened to the doc.

Still, I don't think I could've given up bacon, even knowing what was coming.

"Think we're gonna see the big man, then?" I asked. God or the Devil, I wasn't sure.

"No way." Suit struggled with the rear car door. "I'm not sticking around to meet *anyone*."

"This again," I sighed. His freak-out was sort of funny the first time but was getting old.

"Help me," Suit said, and Headphones grudgingly got up.

"Put your shoulder into it," I said.

"Why are you encouraging them?" Cupcakes asked.

"Way I see it, nothing we can do but try to enjoy the ride, sweetheart."

She frowned as the door cracked open.

Suit turned back to us with some sort of salute. "Sayonara." He stepped off and half a second later stumbled back in, eyes wild.

"Same as the stairs," Headphones guessed and plopped down, pulling out his notebook and pencil and starting to sketch.

"I wish I could've said good-bye to my mom," Cupcakes said out of the blue and got real quiet, turning her head away from us.

"I'm not going to just sit here like cattle carted to the slaughterhouse."

Suit's eyes nearly bugged out of his face. "So I'm not perfect, so what? I deserve this?" He turned and jabbed a finger at the window. "I'd kill you all to get out of here, no question. You'd do the same, don't pretend otherwise. If we're stuck up in Mount Everest and starving, anybody up there would eat their own to survive. Fucking human nature."

"He's losing it all right," I said to no one in particular.

Suit jutted forward and grabbed the knobby pencil from Headphones. He pointed it like a knife at his own neck, gaze out of focus.

"Just do it already so I can have my pencil back," Headphones said. I guessed he was as tired of Suit's shit as I was.

Cupcakes sucked in a breath as Suit rammed the pencil into his throat.

"No blood," I said, a little disappointed. The pencil had popped right out, no mark, nothing.

Suit slapped his neck, calmer. "It hurt anyway. Fuck." He slumped in a seat next to Cupcakes and Headphones resumed drawing. The sketch looked like Cupcakes from this angle but wasn't good enough that I could tell for sure.

More time passed and I closed my eyes. Maybe it was a dream or a hallucination. Maybe if I willed it I could wake the hell up. I tried not to think of anything and pictured a chess board empty of pieces. Symmetrical. Even. No problems, no riddles to solve. Just a blank slate.

An intercom system crackled, and my eyes flew open. We all froze as the static grew louder.

"Passengers who wove themselves badly must depart."

The voice was high-pitched and tinny, coming from all directions and I thought of trumpets.

"What does that mean?" Cupcakes shrieked. "Who are you?"

"I will fuck you up!" Suit shouted up at the ceiling at the same time.

"Next stop: primordial fears."

The intercom went silent after that.

"Primordial fears?" Cupcakes said. "What does that mean?"

"Like fundamental, right," Headphones said. "Fight-or-flight. Like when you see a lion in the jungle, that's a primordial fear to help you survive."

"That doesn't make sense," Cupcakes said. "We're going to fight a lion?"

"I don't deserve this." Suit was ramming his head against the window. He turned to Headphones. "Do you? Are you that evil a person, deep down? So rotten to the core to deserve this?"

"We still don't know what *this* is," Cupcakes said.

"Why us four? Surely we can't be the only ones who sinned. Maybe we died at the same time?" Suit jiggled his knee and rapped against the window for emphasis.

"Could you do us all a favor? Shut the hell up. Just for a few minutes. Or forever." I closed my eyes again when I felt the unmistakable sensation of the train slowing.

"We're stopping," Cupcakes said, voice laced with panic. I couldn't blame her. Panic was fisting my own chest like another heart attack.

The car slid to a stop and the doors hissed open to pitch blackness as the intercom voice crackled again:

"Stop: Primordial fears. Passengers must face themselves and fix their fabric to ascend."

"Fuuuuck me," Suit moaned.

Headphones, I had to give him credit, ventured out first before the rest of us followed, blinking in the shift from florescent lights to darkness.

Headphones inched forward and we followed as our eyes adjusted. At this point I felt more annoyed than anything. Whatever force or being was in charge sure liked dragging things out.

"Just tell us what the deal is already," I said in the darkness.

"Look." Cupcakes jostled next to us. I blinked at a small trickle of light from a narrow passage. The platform we stood on funneled into a weirdly lit cave tunnel.

At least it wasn't red.

We walked through, Headphones, Suit, Cupcakes, and me bringing up the rear.

"God," Cupcakes gagged. The smell was terrible. Like the worst funk you could ever imagine, heated up in a tiny kitchen with your face over the open oven door. Before I could get out of the passage to see what was ahead, something hard slammed into me. It took me a second to figure out what it was.

"Fuck no, no, no," Suit was moaning and shoving, trying to get behind me. But there was nowhere to go; a rock wall had appeared and pressed into my back.

"Get outta here," I snarled and shoved Suit out of my way. I made my way past Cupcakes who had fallen on her knees and Headphones standing there all slack jawed.

That's when I saw it.

An enormous pit yawned out in front of the ledge we stood on. And rising out from the pit—my chest seized up as I recognized the massive shape.

A rat the size of King Kong, stood in the pitch, wearing a goddamn crown and everything. Thousands of normal sized rats ran up and over each other like ocean waves in the pit around the rat king.

"Goddamn why couldn't it be a proper devil?" I had the shakes and my body pressed up against the back of the wall. My stomach slid up my throat again. "Of all the goddamned creatures."

The giant rat, its black eye the size of a bench, looked at me. It squeaked loud as a car horn and waved its paw.

Suit was still screaming.

"This was not what I pictured," Cupcakes said faintly between her hands. "This must be the primordial fear."

"Everyone makes mistakes!" Suit screamed and started hurling stones into the pit. "Die fuckers!" The stones disappeared harmlessly into the pit of rats. "Fucking snakes!"

"Snakes?" I said when the intercom voice boomed again and I saw another subway train behind the rat king, high up and with no obvious way to get to it.

"A stop to fix your fabric."

"Oh no. I think—" Cupcakes stammered, all round eyes. She trembled like it was the dead of winter and looked back at the pit. "I think I'm supposed to jump in. Like be brave enough or strong enough to do it. But I'm really afraid of spiders. It's like a phobia. I can't even look at them. Anything but—"

Just then Cupcakes winked out.

Out of sight.

Out of existence.

"No!" Headphones yelled and something pinched my chest and pricked my eyes.

"Cupcakes, damn," I muttered. I had grown fond of them. What I wouldn't give now to be back at the U station stop or even in the train with them, even if it was for eternity. Anything but the rats.

"Take them!" Suit jabbed a finger at me, spit flying. "Sacrifice them! I'll kill them if you want! Take—" He disappeared mid-shout, the rat king chittering all the while. Its stomach bellowed like a trampoline matted in fur while its crown, darkened gold with dirty jewels, sat crooked between twitching ears. I shuddered and pressed my hands to my ears to drown out its sound, like a chipmunk squeak cranked way up and remixed.

"Why are you doing this?" Headphones dry heaved. "Oh God, I think I'm next. I think...it wants me to jump into the roaches." A look of resolve fell over Headphones. "I'll do it. I'm sorry for everything. I deserve this."

"You crazy?" I jolted forward to stop him but next thing I knew, Headphones ran and jumped, the faded rainbow hood flapping as he fell.

The pit of rats promptly enveloped him, their claws digging in and running over his screaming face before he vanished.

"Let the kid go!" I yelled. A movement behind the rat king's crown caught my eye. Headphones waved from way up, inside the new subway train. His hand pounding the glass, his mouth moving trying to say something.

"OK," I muttered to myself. My stomach started to feel queasy like I was dropping on a roller coaster. "My turn, I guess. You can do this."

I looked at the pit again, the clawed paws and beady eyes undulating in filthy furred bodies. Just watching them made my skin feel like it was sliding off. I tried to breathe through my mouth to avoid the smell of filthy fur and shit.

"Anything else," I said hoarsely. I didn't know what kind of man could face something like that, but it wasn't me, even though I might be dead already. Props to Headphones. "Gimme bugs, fire and damnation. Just not rats."

The voice sounded again from the train behind the rat king, flat and emotionless: *"Primordial fears."*

I hunched over, my knees cracking into the rock. The rats' scampering and squeaking grew louder, and I dug my fingers into my ears. For a wild second I was sure it was an elaborate prank. Had to be. Something to get the old man to jump into a rat pit and film it for all the world to see. My nostrils flared.

"Hell no," I said.

My stomach continued to suck away, and I felt something else: a patch of cold like a draft in January, starting up my legs and under my sweater.

I gritted my teeth as my eyes pricked. I wouldn't think of Pipa and Genevieve or anyone else. This might be the end, the real end, but I had to know one thing. "Did anything matter? What was the point of it all?"

The voice didn't come back. Instead, I heard the new subway start driving off, wheels squeaking. The rat king squirmed above its sea of subjects, their chittering filling my ears as darkness descended.

THE PERFECT GIFT

RICHARD HADN'T EVEN HAD his morning espresso when he read yet another article referring to him as "Drone Guy" in the stream of relentless media covering his every move. Of course, it was Ed, quoted in the *NYT*. *"...he's really more of a drone guy..."*

"You the man," Richard reminded himself aloud through gritted teeth. It was his rallying cry, a mantra to pump himself up before a board meeting or interview with a snarky media personality. Or, in this case, to deal with especially irritating coverage.

Wellspring, his 1200-square-foot automated living/working space, picked up on his agitation and piped in one of his favorite playlists. He focused on the music and the view of Earth from his window as he repeated his mantra to quell his rising blood pressure.

Though he could afford any activity, any whim that crossed his mind, there was nothing quite like looking at Earth from the vantage point of his "space condo." From here it looked like a swipe of paint he could smudge out, a marble he could flick away. Even the darkness around the planet looked different—three dimensional, with depth no painter's colors could capture.

He started to scan the rest of Lacey's PR daily recap (*Morning!!*

Hope you're getting a much-needed break. More media hits below!) when a bang against the outside of the pod made him jump.

He snapped his finger, and Wellspring brightened the rainbow beams of icons and text along its walls, color coded to present him with news and reports. The health and environmental updates showed nothing of note—likely just a small piece of debris colliding with the pod. The life support and fleet statuses pulsed to let him know all was running smoothly, including his hive of chrome drones that floated outside. Through his pod's window, their purple indicators glowed steadily like the reassuring eyes of a pet hound, softening the harshness of black space.

He snapped a finger again and tapped his chin to call up a mirror app on Wellspring's screen. He hadn't included voice automation in his pod; he hated verbal interruptions. Even if someone came to his office when he was back in SF, he'd rather they sit across from his desk and text him so they wouldn't disturb his thoughts. Talking was so ineffectual, so unintelligent.

"You the man, right? Right," Richard said again, squinting at his reflection he could make himself believe it.

Drone Guy! He sipped at a protein pack, trying not to fume. Sebastian and Ed, two guys who consistently ranked as wealthier than him, loved to call him that as if it were some sort of insult, but his code had revolutionized the drone industry, imparting an AI into the machines that blended human-like intelligence with insect-like cooperativity. It made the drones infinitely useful for all sorts of things, including his space jaunts—and without the annoying emotions and questions of a human crew.

He chucked his empty protein pack into the trash compressor, trying not to feel too morose. What Ed, Sebastian and the damned media didn't understand was that he was a *giver*. He had gifted society drones to usher in a new era of technology assistance. And that was just the beginning. He had so many ideas beyond his drone fleet, if only his board would cooperate. But they had given him hell even for sending out a few drones to transmit a "greetings" signal from outside the solar system.

He considered calling Lacey to vent, but she would just remind him that "Drone Guy" was better than the other nicknames the public gave him. "Mr. Handsy," even "Roofie Richard," which was totally unfair and unfounded. It was impossible to date when you were a tech mogul. Of course, women were going to be hysterical, were going to share every little disagreement with the press. After his last debacle in Vegas, Lacey suggested he head up here to distract from news headlines as much as possible.

As he strapped himself into his weight machine, his gaze slid to the nearby bench. His state-of-the-art sex doll, that he had nicknamed Maureen after his ex, sat dutifully, her self-warming silicone legs crossed and fully animatronic mouth resting an eternal pout.

"No one gets me," he told Maureen, going through his reps with particular vigor. "Honestly, it's good to leave Earth's crap behind for a while. You'd hate it—the *diseases*, the *buffoons*, the *politics*. It's enough to make you want to abandon humanity."

His thoughts drifted to a future where people were civil and respected honest-goodness inventiveness when Wellspring quickened the pulse of an orange strip of light above his head, a drone message. He blinked and twirled a finger to magnify the alert on the wall in front of him.

A rhythmic radio signal that didn't match any known cadence.

He sent it to his head of tech, on-call 24/7, and shot off a drone, lucky number 13, closer to investigate and get a second read. The signal appeared to be coming from a group of asteroids that hurtled into the inner solar system on an eccentric orbit, first spotted last week.

Harold, look at this.

Harold's icon blinked in front of him, and together they read the real-time data from 13. A complex signal, layered.

Suggest we call it in, Harold messaged.

Wdy think it is? Richard's heart rate quickened.

Hard to say. Probably should let NASA know. Sending over protocol now.

He should call it in. And he would. But first he would investigate. It was clearly a first of some sort. New material, new type of asteroid.

No, Richard wrote. *Stand by. Going to check it out.*

I really think you shouldn't wait to report—

Richard shut off the feed and stood.

"Drone Guy my ass," he said. He'd be Richard the Revolutionary, Richard the Explorer. He started to send off half the fleet to investigate when another bang—harsh and metallic and louder than typical debris —sounded outside his pod.

"What the hell?"

Two drone updates pulsed rapidly in front of him in urgent red. 3 and 7 hit by something, offline. Two more bangs reverberated through Wellspring.

Like a knocking.

He flicked through his exterior cameras and asked the drones to zero in on the source.

That's when he heard it.

"HELLO."

The hiss came through the air and along his skin, slid up along his ear lobes and along the back of his head like a sweatband.

"Damn space bends," Richard said to himself, the sting of disappointment making his voice whine. Auditory and visual hallucinations were not unheard of in space, along with a host of other physiological oddities, even for experienced travelers. It'd wear off soon enough.

The inside of Wellspring swayed like a bubble about to pop. He squinted and turned his head away as the moon came into view, larger than an imminently colliding pair of headlights. He steadied his breath and pressed his hand into the cool hand rest at the bottom of his display to snap out of it.

"HELLO."

The word again, making him shiver.

One of the drones' cameras finally focused on what had hit the outside of his ship. A blur the size of a goat, hanging onto the side. He zoomed in. A blot with shifting bands of black and white like a static signal. And growing.

"It's not in my head," Richard said once his systems confirmed. "Hooooooly hell!"

First contact. First contact!

"HELLO HELLO."

The word was some kind of auditory and psychic communication coming from the blob outside, *something he could understand.* He had a protocol for this one-in-a-billion event—but who needed protocol in a time like this? He hastily pulled up one of his screens to start recording this iconic moment.

A thousand thoughts buzzed through him in an instant:

What happened in the next few minutes would be the most-watched clip in all of human history.

He would be able to get his space program approved no problem, Board assholes or not.

He wouldn't be known at Drone Guy anymore.

He really would be "The Man."

"This is the first time anyone in humanity has made contact with something outside of Earth," Richard whispered to the recording screen. "I am beyond humble to be experiencing this moment."

He cleared his throat and projected the heady confidence that had gotten him where he was in life. "Hello! Thank you for making contact!"

"HELLO," the voice sang again, and Richard was more used to it this time. He didn't wince, even though it felt like a shard of ice slipping in one ear and out the other. He glanced at the recording. Probably wasn't picking it up if the voice was in his head.

"I'm hearing an extraterrestrial communication coming from this entity outside," Richard narrated.

Whatever the entity was, it didn't seem to be hostile, and he didn't have any kind of weapons anyway—why would he in his space office?

"Hello! What are you? Do you…um…come in peace? I sure do." Richard spread his hands open wide to demonstrate in case the entity could see. He could feel it there, like an audience enshrouded in shadows, curiously watchful.

"VISITOR. HELLO." The entity said. With a jolt, Richard thought of the drones he had sent off to transmit a welcome signal before the board clamped down on him.

"Holy—the drones found you." Richard snapped his fingers and laughed, shakily. "Yes! I knew it!" He spelled it out for the video clip.

"*My* drones discovered you, brought you here. Please let me welcome you on behalf of planet Earth."

He bowed his head for effect.

"*GIFT. GIFT.*" The voice seemed to come from outside the spacecraft but also inside his head, like he was listening to the same concert in an amphitheater and through headphones.

"Um…" Richard wracked his brain and tried to think, though his heartbeat was going fast enough to make his hands shake. *You the man.* "You want a gift? Of course. You can have a drone."

It trilled a no, like a hundred cicadas, through his temples.

"*GIFT. DESIRE,*" it said. It seemed to be learning, the words coming easier. "*FOR YOU. FOR EARTH.*"

Richard hadn't gotten where he was by not getting details nailed down in concrete agreements. "OK, that is really cool of you. What kind of gift though?"

"*YOUR DESIRE.*"

He opened his mouth and paused as a sliver of doubt ran through him. Who was he anyway, to be having first contact, to be accepting a gift like an ambassador of Earth?

He pushed through any doubt. He wouldn't be as successful as he was if he gave into insecurities, if he listened to every little voice of hesitancy in him that told him he'd only ever be Drone Guy.

Why shouldn't he be the one to accept it? He was a prime specimen of human, he was a good enough representative as any. Sure, he wasn't perfect, he lost his temper sometimes, but he was working on it. Ultimately, he was trying to make himself and the world a better place, and that had to count for something. And he was a way better representative of Earth than Sebastian or Ed. Ed wouldn't hesitate. He smirked thinking of Ed jealously watching this moment.

"Yes," Richard said humbly. "I accept the gift, on behalf of humanity."

Silence. He tried to mimic the feeling of the words from the entity as a thought he projected: *I accept!*

It worked.

"*WE CREATE. DESIRE,*" the entity said, sounding pleased. The words vibrated along his skull. "*YOU WANT? LIKE?*"

He nodded and spoke loudly so the camera would hear. "First contact, mainly through a sort of psychic-auditory conversation. The entity is offering me a gift, thank you so much. For Earth I wish for um, peace of course. Prosperity. Order. Scientific Advancement. Let's say a peaceful agreement. Maybe you want to come back down with me?"

But the words didn't seem to resonate with the entity. Instead, he felt the buzzing in his mind, like it was searching.

"WANT? WANT? WANT?"

The question dug into him, excavating his thoughts, like a beetle had scurried through his ear and nestled behind his eyes. Nevertheless, he managed a smile for the camera as he waited. The back of his neck prickled like someone about to breathe on him. He turned.

A shadow had gathered in the corner of his pod, right on the other side of where the blurry image of the entity was captured. Whatever it was, it was coming in through the ship's hull, pooling into the size of a human.

Richard shot backwards. "What in the hell!"

"*GIFT*," the entity explained.

It was the shape of a goddamn person. Gray and gelatinous. He gestured for Wellspring to follow and continue to record.

"I, uh, there's something in here with me," Richard narrated. He inched forward toward the gray blob. It emanated warmth. Warm like a bath. Warm like flesh.

Stay calm for the video. You the man.

"*YOU THE MAN*," the entity agreed and again dove into his memories, a little buzzing static that wound from one ear to another, searching. Memories bubbled up, random moments at parties and dates and events, all the times he felt like no one understood him, like he was completely alone in this world. How Sebastian and Ed treated him like some hack, like his work and ideas were second rate. His dad's funeral, his mom shaking her head at the idea of drone fleets. All the women who broke up with him. All the board members that doubted him.

The entity watched, greedy as a kid in a toy store.

"Maybe stop," Richard said.

"*PERFECT GIFT,*" it crowed.

Richard blinked and looked back at the blob. He stuffed a fist in his mouth to stop from screaming when it—*she*—looked up. The blob's face was a crisscross of white and black, like something half stitched, flickering in and out like a bad movie. Milky bulging sacks passed for eyes. White flecks peppered over the bubbling skin, mottled, reminding him of a fungal infection. Breasts like dirty water balloons swung on either side of a bony sternum as the creature became sharper and more defined.

The approximation of a woman did not have a mouth. She lifted a hand toward him. Her fingers flopped, like dead snakes attached to a limb.

"*GIFT. PERFECT.*" The entity said. It reminded Richard of an eager first date, trying to impress. "NOT LONELY. TOGETHER."

His thoughts hit staccato notes, trying to make sense of things, like two dozen TV channels blazing at once.

The woman-creature moved, hand on its hip, its grotesque pose somehow assured. It flipped nonexistent hair. When she tilted her head provocatively, all the breath went out of him. Her posture was a mirror image of Maureen's, before the breakup. She had almost been the one.

The creature straightened. What looked like painted-on eyeballs, wide and flat, stared. Fish-lips pushed out from above her chin, sealed but for a small puckering hole, pink and fleshy. She stood silent, reminding him of how Maureen would go all quiet and judgmental when he said something she didn't like.

"*LIKE?*" The entity asked.

"No!" Richard shouted and shoved the memories away. "I do not like, this is pretty fucked up, honestly. 'A' for effort, but maybe we could stop now, no offense."

Once again, he was completely misunderstood, even by a freaking psychic alien.

"*GIFT GIFT GIFT,*" the voice insisted.

"Read this: fuck off," Richard said. Maybe not the best approach to first contact but this entity—whatever it was—was screwing with him. Enough was enough. He tensed, red creeping into his sight. He readied a fist. He'd pummel this creature if he had too, drag the body back to sell to DARPA to dissect.

The creature flickered again, its features becoming inchoate, its edges blurring as it morphed through variations of its form. It twirled extensions that looked like curls, reminding him of Mackenzie, his first girlfriend in college. The creature shifted again, raising its hands as if pleading, something in its sharp cheekbones and sloping forehead now making him think of that girl in Vegas, of the blood smeared across his knuckles and satin sheets. He didn't even remember her name, but that was the night the press almost found out, the night he almost lost everything. The next time the figure flickered, it smoothed into chrome curves, its eyes purple pinpoints.

"There, stop!" Richard shouted. The creature paused and he stared.

It was a secret project he had only dreamt of doing, now manifesting right in front of him in the metallic sweeps of boobs, the tassels of silver hair, the attentive purple gaze.

An honest-goodness drone woman. All the curves, the intelligence, the clarity, with none of the problems.

"Yes," Richard said faintly and stepped closer. She positively gleamed. Her violet eyes glowed, large and flat. No emotion, except attentiveness. Ready to serve. Ready to love. His mind raced—an alien-infused AI would be light years ahead of his tiny drone fleet. He could study it, understand it to bring about the next-level, killer-app version of drones while he was praised across the globe for being the liaison to a powerful extraterrestrial entity.

And a drone woman like this—that held uncanny intelligence, that actually *listened*—would finally understand him.

"Yes, this is a good gift," he whispered and, damn, felt his eyes prickle with the power of this moment. He didn't even care what the clip caught.

"TOGETHER," the entity buzzed as the drone woman swept toward him, arms open.

Her eyes blinked, so alert—so *ready*—

The drone woman brought her puckering lips to his, crushing his cheekbones and nose like a face full of cement.

Richard sputtered and tried to knee her in the crotch to get her to back off, but she didn't relent. Steel-like limbs crushed him in an embrace. The creature's face mashed into his again, her pecking lips subtle as a jabbing screwdriver.

"Damn it! You're hurting me!" he managed through the blood streaming into his mouth. The ropes of her hair fell heavy as tire chains on his shoulders. "Stop...why aren't you listening." He tried to project the thought to the entity, but pain stunned him, splintering his focus while his shoulder blades popped.

"*GIFT. FOR EARTH,*" the entity said. "*TOGETHER. NOT LONELY.*"

The creature squeezed, making everything in him short circuit. He heard the sound of a car running over branches, and realized it was his bones. His skin ripped easy as recycled tissue paper when she hugged him.

"Stop...please..." Richard's words devolved into a gurgled scream as the drone woman's hips ground into his, a car rim smashing his genitals into a pulpy mush. He turned his head as he disassociated, the pain a wave that swept away his breath and thought. Through his failing vision, he glimpsed specks against the black of space out of his window. He struggled to make them out, not believing what he was seeing.

"*GIFT.*" The entity said, endlessly pleased. "*TOGETHER.*"

A grid of drone women—thousands, maybe more—hung outside of his pod. Not just floating but moving in formation through space. Like his drones, he realized before his vision darkened.

All sailing toward the tiny blue Earth.

UNREST

THE CAR ROLLS TO A STOP, positioned squarely in front of the Holland Cemetery gates as though it's a natural parking spot. Furrows of hills studded with tombstones like goosebumps rise behind the gate.

I scrutinize Henry's sharp cheekbones in the twilight from the passenger seat. I know about the switchblade tucked inside his pocket, probably icy against his thigh through the fabric. I smooth my hands over my tights, trying to ignore the cemetery's presence, watchful as a disapproving parent wondering what's taking so long for me to come inside.

"Sorry, Lada, babe. We're out of gas." Henry shrugs.

It's true, this I know. I also know he's planned it. His breath is quickening, his back has straightened—like a hunter that just caught a whiff of potential prey.

"What should we do now?" I say and preen, the good girlfriend. Deep in my core, I hum at the nearness to the cemetery, desperate for me to come inside, but I stuff those feelings down. Some things can't be rushed.

And a part of me hopes, maybe this time will be different.

"Walk, I guess. We'll have to cut through the cemetery." Henry gives me a lopsided grin under his sandy hair. Attentive, relaxed, charismatic. I never thought I would have enjoyed our week together so much. I had been, for the first time, *alive*: humming along to street music as we snuggled on a bench; watching the first snowfall swirl past the blur of moonlight and into his hair; scorching my tongue on fresh-blazed mozzarella from the stone-oven pizza place nearby, hearing the squeals of children tearing through the park—all of it, razor sharp, technicolored. And threading through each memory, Henry's warm embrace, like a drug I can't get enough of.

As we get out of the car, I sneak a look at his face, which is a mask expertly concealing the storm within. Most people don't see it, but I am acutely aware of the anger that makes up every fiber of his being. We file through the small, broken, gated door next to the cemetery sign and shame wells in me. How could I have fallen for such a monster?

Because you're a monster too, something whispers back.

"So, it's safe here, right?" I say casually. A dozen crows watch from a scraggly tree. The closest one tilts its head, fixes its beady eyes on me. I will it to be silent.

Henry drinks up my naiveté. He thinks I'm new to town and I don't know better.

"Of course. Just us and the birds." He zips his vest and slugs an arm across my shoulders. The heat diffuses through my back, across my throat and down my chest, awakening flesh held together by icy winds, midnight moons and the soft sobbing of someone, always out of reach.

It's almost time.

The hopelessness hangs like a fog here. I breathe it in. Despair is what the dead infuse in the graveyard, this is to be expected. But nipping at the corners of the gloom is something that cannot remain, the thing I'm here to fix, the thing that Henry brings.

Rage.

"Hey, let's stop up here," Henry says as we bound up the next hill.

Don't, I think. But he continues.

"You know, I'm sort of glad we had a chance to walk through here. There's something I want to tell you." Henry's voice is too eager. The tombstones lean in, an audience straining to hear. The ground below me grumbles, restless.

Soon, I tell it, half-heartedly.

We finally reach the spot. The hill looks unremarkable, but the wind blows a little icier here, the patches of dirty snow never seem to melt. Here, memories bubble like an infected cyst. I look down at my muddy boots, thinking of all the women who have stood in this place before. Their screams still reverberate in the ground, tearing at any stitches the graveyard tries—and fails—to bind, time and time again.

"Lada, babe. I know it's early in our relationship. But I really feel...like I love you. Is that crazy?" Henry stops and spins toward me, framed by two looming blocks of marble and slate, illegible in the dark air. He trails a finger along my cheek, making me shiver and waver. His eyes are intent—he *means* it, in his twisted definition of love. Even though I have become what would please him, the fact that he chooses me for his own makes my breath catch.

"I love you too." I suck in the air, willing its coldness to shock some sense into me. Clouds flow like ink above us.

Henry's eyes are too bright. His love for me has reached a tipping point, spilling into his sacred pain. I can almost feel it there, the beating core at his center that drew me to him. It feels like a sack of bones hardened into obsidian chards, tucked into a tiny black hole where his heart should be.

"I got you this." Henry holds up a locket. A simple golden heart punctured with a garnet. I know he's given the same to girls before me. Six so far, all in their early 20s. All with longish hair, a way of talking that is more sighing, and a fondness for skirts. All missing now, their remains stuffed under his favorite tomb, where wilting wildflowers grow along the cracked limestone.

I nod, bracing for the inevitable and remind myself I'm here to do one job.

Remember what he is, I tell myself. *What you are.*

We're both creatures of anguish, brought together by fate, neither of us deserving of love. Still, I hesitate. I'm bound to him, I am who I am because of his hate and sadness. But maybe there's a chance for us to both be more. If he changes, *now*, we can continue beyond the graveyard gates to live.

"Thank you. It's beautiful," I say, and I mean it. He beams while I fasten the necklace.

Now, now, now, the cemetery urges. I ignore it, containing myself for just a little longer. The graveyard hisses in anger.

My hope crashes when I see how Henry's gaze is glassy, the look of someone in the full throes of their psychosis. It's like a switch has been thrown.

"How about a kiss?" His breathing is faster now, his posture too taut.

I hesitate, remembering the brush of his lips to mine, the jolt of sweet electricity that runs through my mouth.

Even though I'm expecting it, I'm not ready for how fast he is as the knife comes out, how deftly he presses it to my neck. I try to pull back, but his other hand has expertly wrapped around the back of my shoulder.

"Don't fight it, Lada," he says, almost monotone, as if he's been coerced into auditioning for a play. He is measured, surgical, though he's panting.

"Henry, you don't have to do this," I gasp. I don't know what made him this way. Perhaps something in his brain needs rebalancing, or some unspeakable childhood trauma broke him beyond repair. But maybe if I say the right lines, I can untangle the knot of his sickness, pull the thread out of him.

Then we can leave this place together.

The crows' wings slice the darkness overhead, trying to get my attention. The winds moan in frustration.

"Please," I say. "I know what you've done. You can stop it, now."

Henry's eyes darken but he doesn't say anything.

"You find a way to bring all of your girlfriends here," I continue. The petite woman with the fondness for purple eyeshadow and library books; the brunette in the homemade skirt and her grandmother's hand-me-down pearls. The blade is cold but not as cold as my skin. "And they all go missing afterwards."

"I didn't do anything," he says but the lie breaks his fragile words, so he tries again, this time sounding like a whining child caught with a forbidden candy. "I can't...help it."

I had seen it all before I became Lada, seen through the air and the trees and the stones how cleanly he split open their necks. I had drowned as their blood soaked into our grass, I had howled with the winds as their bodies were stuffed into our grounds. Each of the fine gold links of each of the necklaces crushed underfoot, embedded into the earth like infected splinters.

But really it was the rage that had woken me. The girls' screams entangled with his fury had sunk deep into the earth, echoing again and again so there was no rest, *never any rest.*

Finally, the cemetery drew me up from the land, coalesced into Lada by the dead with a simple duty: to heal this scar, to rid us of the parasite that had soiled our hallowed dirt. It is my first time as a human, made up of the fragments of the dead's memories, traits, abilities. I am something the graveyard has constructed, birthed as a last desperate act to grant peace.

"You have to stop coming here," I plead. "Let the dead rest. Say you will."

Muscles spasm across Henry's face like an electric storm and he shakes his head.

"*Why?*" My voice is hoarse. "Of all places, why torment the dead with more death?"

"They're most afraid here." He's so quiet I can barely hear him. "Fear makes them most alive."

NOW NOW NOW the graveyard is screaming. It can't wait: the ground rumbles and splits next to him, stretching into a chasm that is exactly his body-length. A slab of granite emerges from the dirt, gleaming like a tooth.

Henry looks over at the new gravestone, a frown deepening the lines along his mouth as he tries to make sense of it. His hands loosen a fraction of their strength and I yank away, pivoting free before he jabs the knife in response.

He stares at me in astonishment before his jaw tightens. He expects me to run and is ready to chase. Instead, I reach out, both hands open.

"Don't take this from me. From us," I beg. Everything in me recoils at the thought of the murdered bodies, their bones mangled on top of each other in their makeshift graves, but then I think of his arms. His eyes like lanterns. How his laughter sends shivers along my ear lobe, my neck.

"I want to stay Lada. Stay with you. I *love* you. Even after all you've done," I say. "We could leave this place, start a new life."

I'm not sure if the graveyard will allow it but I sense it watching, waiting. If Henry never comes here again, maybe we can both be free.

His face opens and for a second, I can almost see what he could have been: his potential for kindness, his clever way of seeing patterns and articulating them as beautifully as a poet. It's all there, almost concrete. A second later, the real Henry takes over. I draw back as I see the clumps of red fury, like barbed hooks, embed into every piece of him, inseparable from his core.

His face twists, snarling as he dives forward with the knife again. It nicks the edge of my necklace instead. The fragments of the gold chain twinkle in the moonlight, like half a dozen wishes, extinguished suddenly.

My love is not enough.

I sob aloud as the realization hits me, sharp like a piece of glass in my gut.

And he will never let the graveyard be.

Now, it really was time. I rise and shed my façade. It is disconcerting to be so big, so airy after the comfort of boundaries, the comfort of contained flesh. Now I cannot feel, I cannot leave.

I can only serve.

Henry's face gapes and then contorts into panic.

"Lada! Lada!" Henry is screaming louder than all his victims together. His eyes bulge as he looks up at me. He stabs his knife into me again and again. I only feel tiny jolts, like static electricity.

I am between ethereal and solid now, made of white and gray gossamer, loosely bound together in the rough conglomeration of the bones below. Around my skeletal head stream threads that shimmer all the textures of his dead girlfriends' hair—a reminder to him. I scream at him for all the girls that can't. I scream at him for myself, for the chance to live that was so close, but gone.

The rage feels good, a release. I still feel love—oh and the *sorrow*—all raw, uncontained by human limits even as some threads of Lada still cling to me.

Henry is trying to crawl away, bellowing like an animal. I float forward, cradle him in what approximates hands, emaciated branches of fingers.

"Time to rest," I say, my words a summoned wind.

Maybe death would give him some respite, a chance to start again.

I embrace him as gently as I can in my form, but he is writhing too much, and I accidentally crunch bones like sticks. His cries turn animal-like, wounded and afraid, and I blink back the memory of tears.

I place him in the pit. He struggles but the earth eagerly closes over him, smothering his frame. His hands strain out of the dirt, clawing at the air. I toss the broken necklace onto the mound and a fissure of pain seems to cleave me in two.

At least now we can heal, I think. Maybe I will be called forth again, someday, if the graveyard needs me. For now, I grow more ephemeral, my matter curling into the branches, flitting into the crumbling brown dirt, between straining earthworms and dung beetles. I'm unspooling; I try to hold onto the memory of warmth on a park bench, the feeling of laughter bubbling up in my throat, and the rush of food and music and snowflakes and clasped hands. My tears are condensed dew, shivering orbs on the matted grass.

Henry's soul will release in a glittering cloud like shattered quartz. Traces of his rage will join the echo of the girls' screams, intermingling in the soil. Like everyone in the graveyard, hints remain of who they had been, sunk into the terrain like a stain.

Henry's shouts are growing fainter now, muffled.

It will be the last screams the graveyard hears.

THE NIGHT CALL

DYLAN SAT on a towel on the roof, mulling over his high and chugging one of his dad's Miller Lites. He'd swiped the beer from the fridge before climbing out the kitchen window and onto the fire escape, leaving behind the tension that spewed from his dad and wound around his mom's voice, pushing it to a higher and higher pitch. Eventually her voice would get so high it'd crack, the tightly held threads spooling out an airborne poison through the apartment. Their constant fighting would always lead to one of them finding him to start up the same crap: *maybe* if he was better at school, *maybe* if he helped out more, they wouldn't be so stressed.

But up here Dylan couldn't hear his mom's voice crack, couldn't hear their unfair accusations. Up here he was alone in his dark oasis, the generators muting the shouting from inside and the honking from below.

He pulled out the butterfly knife his dad had given him for his 11th birthday and flipped it open, admiring the way the moonlight glimmered on the blade he'd sharpened earlier. The click-clack of the two yellow handles as he flipped the knife around in the basic backhand twirl move soothed him. Funny, it always drove his mother crazy. *You better not*, she'd say, her face furrowing in anger.

Dylan took a swig of the beer and spun the knife faster, flipping it around his fingers with ease. He practiced his new combo – where he flipped the handles, tossed up the knife and caught it—a sick move that would scare off his classmates if he needed it. He threw the knife again and again, handles flashing. *Faster, faster.* Finally, the blade slipped down past his fingers and into his wrist, spilling the Miller Light all over.

"Damn it!"

He strained in the moonlight but couldn't see how bad the cut was. It hurt like hell. He cursed again even though the pain felt good, grounding him. Some of his anger seeped out with the dark blood that spread across the concrete roof. He pulled the towel from under him and pressed it against the cut, trying to relax as he waited for the pain to stop.

Above him, a dark spot on the moon like an eye leered. A valley, his science teacher had said during their astronomy unit. Dry seas, full of nothing but rocks and dust the color of bleached bones. Sea of Serenity, Sea of Tranquility. Yesterday they had learned about Pluto and its moons, Charon, Styx, Nix and—he couldn't remember the rest. He pictured them, rocky orbs covered in ashes, hurtling through space in never-ending loops. Like his own life, a never-ending loop he couldn't escape. Like a loop, his thoughts fell to how easy it would be to keep his eyes on the moon and walk, taking the final, single step over the roof. He'd reach out for the sky before gravity took hold and ended his loop so he wouldn't have to go through another day of numbness, of boredom, of the barely contained rage that simmered in the house like the smell of last night's take-out.

Maybe tonight would be the night.

Dylan's vision blurred and he saw what looked like a thread appear and unravel itself from one of the moon's dead seas. He blinked but the white thread was still there, slowing sliding down like paint dripping from the sky.

"Insane," he muttered to himself. It must be the weed, stronger than he had thought it was, playing with his eyes. Dylan blinked a few more times but the white beam grew. He sat up, pulling off his baseball cap so he could get a clear view.

"You're so high," Dylan said aloud. What else could explain that crazy beam, which was widening, shimmering like a river slowly pouring down from the sky. A darker smudge moved down with it.

A figure.

But that was impossible. Dylan rubbed his eyes with the hand that didn't hurt, pressing his fingers against his lids so hard his eyeballs moved in their sockets. When he looked again, the figure was much closer.

The figure was a *she*: her knees pumped up and down like she was marching in reverse or stepping down a ladder. A body suit or iridescent paint coated her faint skin. One second, she was in the distance; but after the next blink she was only a few dozen feet away. *Impossible.*

And the light—it wasn't a beam anymore, but a spotlight shining right on the edge of the roof of his building. The figure stepped down in the center of the glowing circle, placing one bare foot on the roof, followed by the other.

There must have been more than weed in that joint.

Whatever the girl wore—paint or cloth—was luminescent enough to blur the lines of her body. A fluff of dark hair was pulled into a bun on her head. Eyes, round and wide as a doll's, glanced at him.

"Did you just…did you just climb over from that building?" Dylan could have sworn it was from the moon but that was insane. His vision was off, he couldn't see straight.

The spotlight behind her had faded. Now it looked like a glow-in-the-dark net leading up between the two buildings.

Just a painted rope. But the way it rippled in the darkness looked more like sparkling smoke suspended in the air.

"I'm sort of an acrobat," the girl said, her voice warbly and faint. She pulled her forehead close to her straight knees, her hair floating around her head like a black halo as she stretched.

Dylan relaxed a tiny bit. Of course. There were plenty of performing artists in the city. His eyes had been tripping on him. He was still high, and it was dark, and he hadn't been feeling that well anyway. He pulled his baseball cap back on and repositioned the sticky towel on his wound.

"Uhh," he said. He started to stand but a wave of dizziness insisted he sit. His cut gave an angry pulse, and he pressed the damp cloth harder against it. "What's your name?"

"Anything you want it to be." She didn't say it suggestively, but rather matter-of-factly as she straightened.

She was trying to be mysterious, Dylan figured, but two could play that game. He kept his face as bored and uninterested as possible and said the first thing that popped into his head.

"Cool. I'll call you Serenity," Dylan said. "What's with the rope ladder? Performance art?"

Serenity wound her hands out in front of her, her fingers outstretched. She reminded Dylan of one of those yoga girls he saw downtown, toting their yoga mats in bags across their backs like trophies of superiority. He scowled a little but couldn't help but watch as she raised her arms out to the sides.

"We should get going." Serenity lifted one foot straight up and out, parallel to the ground and stretched her arm above it like a ballerina. Her whole body was like one long muscle. She didn't move like anyone he'd ever seen; something about her was off but he couldn't place it.

Acrobat, he reminded himself. "Why are you here?" Dylan asked, sharper than he meant. His wrist gave a throb again and he ignored it.

She smiled, and tiny claws of fear nipped at Dylan. Looking at her knotted his stomach, so he glanced away at the generator humming frantically behind him, at the soft clouds billowing past the moon. When he turned back, her leg and arms were still suspended, a statue. Her eyes settled on him, shining like the shell of a huge beetle.

"Are you afraid of me?" Serenity whispered. She had some sort of odd inflection in her voice; it didn't sound quite like the Bronx or Queens or even Jersey. Her eyes slid to his knife. "It can be scary. I came to help."

"What? I don't need help."

"You like tricks?" She arched her spine back, back, as if she had no bones at all, until it was like her upper body had disappeared as her forehead bowed to the ground and her face turned up and peered at him from between her knees.

Serenity giggled, and some of Dylan's fear fell away. One of her shoulders twitched and she sighed.

"What the hell. How did you do that?" he said. "Oh, right, acrobat."

"Your turn." Serenity looked pointedly at his butterfly knife from her upside-down position. Last week during lunch, a new girl, Marie, had watched from the next table as Dylan did a quick combo spin, his blade slipping like liquid between his fingers. Marie had gasped and then stared down at her sandwich, smiling a little.

Dylan held up his butterfly knife in the moonlight with the hand that didn't hurt, opening and locking the blade into place.

Serenity watched attentively from her odd position, so he mustered up some effort and tried one of his easier tricks, a toss and catch. But his fingers were wet, and the knife slid from his hand back into his lap.

"Now," Serenity said, shifting on her hands and feet to move closer to him, her back still looped like a rubber band. The shuffling reminded him of a spider. "We have to go."

"What is that?" Dylan jabbed a thumb toward the netting, which was still there, like a quivering rope of moonlight. His arm hurt so bad. "I'm just gonna close my eyes for a few minutes."

Serenity's eyes flicked to the side. "We have to get going. It's a long way but I'll help you."

"You're a freak," Dylan said. Anger swelled in him, focusing his vision. "I don't want to go anywhere with you."

His words seemed to hang in the night air, hollow. He thought of his parents downstairs, who probably hadn't even noticed he was gone. They pretended to be so mature, he thought, but really they just reminded him of two dogs circling, waiting for a chance to bite each other—or him. Maybe it *would* be better if he went with Serenity.

She shuffled over to him in her strange posture, stopping a few inches away, and opened her lips. Dylan thought he'd smell her breath, but he smelled nothing.

"Come on now. What's done is done," she breathed. Dylan felt the words on his face, like the tiny legs of a ladybug, picking their way over his cheek. "We have to hurry."

"Your crazy net? No way. How do I know that thing's not going to fall apart?"

Serenity's head moved back from between her legs as she straightened to a standing position. Her shoulder blades lifted and dropped like thin ceramic plates. She took a playful jump forward and smiled. He noticed again how her head was too round for her loose limbs, limbs which hardly seemed attached to her. He also noticed that her teeth, the same shade as her skin, were slightly pointed.

Carnival freak, he thought with a shiver. He should be grossed out, but there was something hypnotic about her half smile in the dark, the air that lifted in a breeze. The breeze got stronger, whipping into a wind and Serenity's smile faded. It was dark, the moon blotted out somehow.

"We have to go now," Serenity said with a note of urgency that made Dylan's chest tighten. "They're coming."

"Who? The cops? My parents?" Dylan struggled to stand but his whole arm felt numb, his body too heavy.

Serenity's eyes gleamed black, the moon white above her. "Please."

"I'm not getting up," Dylan snapped. "What the hell is going on? Tell me, Serenity."

"There are...predators. Between here and there. Then and now."

"What are you talking about?" Dylan did finally get to his feet then, and it was a Herculean effort. "What do they want?"

Her next words, breathed so softly, sent a shiver down his spine.

"Like any predators, they're hungry."

Dylan nodded, ready to take her hand. He wondered if he would feel anything at all if he touched her and held his breath as the space between their fingertips shrank. But her small hand seemed warm and normal. His own palm was covered with sweat, but she didn't seem to mind. It was so dark now, he could barely see anything.

Serenity's hand tightened around his and the net flared brighter. Just as quickly she let him go, glancing up and baring her tiny sharp teeth. "It's too late!"

A whoosh rose. Dylan froze.

Something was watching them.

Whatever it was flapped above them, a shadow blotting the sky that made a sound like a speaker system gone bad. And the smell—he nearly gagged—it was a thousand times worse than rows of garbage bags in the summer in Manhattan.

Before he could shout, the shadow flapped. A cape, a bird—no, something much larger. Nothing that big could fly, nothing that big had black wings like that that took up half the sky.

His mind worked too slowly to reason even as Serenity screamed at it to go.

The creature swooped and landed, sending up a waft that made Dylan's eyes water. It loomed, human-shaped but large, and as opaque as Serenity was luminescent.

That wasn't the worst part.

Dylan could make out small gray faces nestled into its wings.

Tiny, furrowed brows the size of children's dolls glared at him, their mouths gaping in silent fury. His first thought was that they were carnies like she was, chasing after her, or some kind of special effects suit. But he could see the faces were stitched, somehow, onto the wings.

He scooted backwards as best he could, anything to get away from that thing. The creature turned and two white orbs the size of tennis balls fixed on him.

Eyes.

In what passed for a face that he could only register as shark-like. Its smooth and featureless face stretched back from a too-wide mouth, a mouth he didn't want to see smile or move or *open*—

"Holy…" Dylan started to shout but sound wasn't working, his words were sapped away in the wind. He scooted backwards on the roof as the creature tunneled toward him.

Serenity shrieked, an angry, high-pitched sound, and the thing veered toward her instead. Its wings enveloped her like a blanket, the tiny gray faces screeching as they bit into her. Serenity shrieked again, her glow rapidly fading.

"No!" Dylan picked up his knife and hurled it with his good hand. The blade, glowing in the moonlight, shot over Serenity's shoulder to sink into the creature's eyeball.

The creature howled and the faces screamed.

Dylan pressed his hand to his ear and ducked, hoping the sound wouldn't burst his eardrums. But the attack gave Serenity the second she needed to dart free. Her foot shot out in a graceful spinning kick and sent the creature plummeting over the side of the building, taking the butterfly knife with it.

Serenity stood in front of him, her hair a mess and thin arms trembling.

"Is it gone?" Dylan gasped. No matter how much air he sucked in, it felt like he couldn't breathe. "Crap that was—I don't even know. Is it really gone?"

"For now." Serenity's suit or skin was so bright he had to squint. Her voice grew stronger. "They can sense when someone is about to leave. Are you ready?"

The moonlit net flared, blinding, made of fluid twisting grooves. It reminded him of the ridges in tree trunks or leaves fluttering high overhead, scattering the sunlight.

Dylan took Serenity's hand and felt a trickle of a feeling. Pride. He had fought off something unreal, something he couldn't begin to name.

She gripped his hand and helped him up, leading him toward the moon. The net and Serenity gave off an incandescence that was nearly intoxicating, that made the pain in Dylan's heart and arm disappear, made him feel like he was dissolving into a warm bath.

He understood: he'd finally get to visit the moon like he wanted.

"Wait," Dylan pulled back. He thought of Marie at lunch and pictured themselves sitting together in science class, sketching patterns of constellations. He thought of his parents' faces in the rare moments when they weren't fighting. If he handled some supernatural beast, surely he could handle his own less-than-ideal loop.

"I think I want to stay here." Dylan let go of her hand, the warm sheen slipping off of him and the familiar pain returning. "Can I do that? Stay?"

Serenity glanced to the edge of the roof, where the thing had fallen. "Not usually." She smiled, her pointed teeth not that sharp after all. "But you can this time."

He closed his eyes as the light brightened, feeling her slip away.

When Dylan opened them again, she was gone. He gasped, and the sound turned to a moan as the pain in his arm returned. He glanced down.

"Damn!" The wound was bleeding way worse than he thought. He might need stitches. He wrapped the edge of his shirt around his wrist and hurried to the window.

Before he went back inside, he looked up at the moon. Ordinary, distant.

A sense of peace spread through him as he kept looking, until he could make out the dry seas, the ridges and valleys. All stretched out in a landscape of white and silver, that gleamed like the blade of a knife.

BETTER HALVES

SOMETHING WASN'T QUITE RIGHT, but Anne couldn't place it. At first, she thought it was the weather, casting a gloomy sheen over their summer beach trip.

"Stupid New England," she said. An apt belated birthday present, she thought sourly. A face peered at her through the passenger window reflection: her own, frowning and fragmented against the rain flecks.

"It's a week out of the city," said Derick, ever the optimist. "We can get lobsters."

The GPS spoke up and her husband yanked the wheel. A small wooden sign with the inn's name in white script clattering against a post barely lit by the headlights, the first sign of a town they had seen since passing the iHop half an hour back.

"But I wanted to take photos," she said, her heart sinking as the house came into view through the mist. It was—well—*older* than she had expected, with peeling paint and raindrops caught trembling in spider webs along the top of the front door. Flowers on the nearby trellis sagged as if their dark colors were about to stream off like paint.

Inside, a carpet studded with roses bloomed at their feet before running up a narrow stairwell. "Welcome! Honeymoon suite top floor in back. Breakfast at 8," read a note on the counter, pinned down by a key on a wooden keychain.

Upstairs, Derick bumped into Anne as she stopped at the room's entrance. "What's wrong?"

"*This* is the honeymoon suite?" she said. The room was dim, the bed high with overstuffed lace pillows that her grandmother would've liked. Small watercolors of boats and colonial houses peppered the floral wallpaper.

"It's not so bad."

"It's not great," Anne said, dropping her bag and stepping over to a vanity desk below an enormous, ornate mirror. "Maybe it's the feng shui."

She leaned down to check her hair and stopped, entirely caught off guard by what she saw. It wasn't the unpleasant but familiar sensation of seeing time tug away at skin and flesh that felt immortal. No, something else was off—something in the way the light peeled away at the edges of the mirror, like several of her reflections lay directly behind the first. The boundaries of her edge begin to blur when—

"Look what they left for us."

Anne's eyes slid away and toward her husband, who raised a wooden board with crackers and cubes of cheddar toward her.

"Nice," she said, and her voice sounded hollow. "Let's go to bed."

The bed was soft and warm despite its old-fashioned look, and she started to feel relaxed for the first time all day until Derick nuzzled her. She turned onto her back. "Stomachache," she breathed and waited until she heard his breath grow slow and long, asleep.

Like clockwork, Anne's surge of resentment faded to a familiar, throbbing guilt. She knew he wanted a family. She did too, in theory. They had agreed to wait until her 34th birthday, enough time for her to start up an online photography shop and market herself to galleries. But of course, things had gotten in the way and now her time was up.

Maybe during maternity leave she'd have time to pursue projects that always seemed to be on hold. Her mother's voice floated to her, sentences Anne had heard too many times.

You'll feel different when you have a baby.
Art school isn't a career.

You are so lucky to have Derick.

It has all worked out well enough so far. Derick was sweet and she had a decent career in banking, on a fast track for a promotion. Having a kid would probably be fine too. So why was she on the brink of hyperventilating?

Anne squashed down the stew of panic into a more manageable ball of unease as she sat up, reaching for her water bottle. From the bed, she could make out her silhouette in the mirror to her left, coarsely granular as the curtains sighed, scattering moonlight around the room.

From here, she looked like a nymph who had climbed up the trellis and crept into their room, feral and damp from the outdoors. Or like a mermaid who had just gained legs for the night and ran across the sand and grass, drawn to the glint of the mirror.

I'm tired, Anne thought and laid herself down next to her husband.

The inn manager, Betty, served them breakfast, plopping down plates with scrambled eggs and slightly crooked corn muffins.

"Do you like the room?" Betty murmured. She didn't look much older than Anne but wore an old-fashioned long green skirt and brown apron and too-thick glasses.

Derick nodded. "Not bad. How old is this place?"

"1750. It used to be a mansion. Survived two fires." Betty gave a pale grin as she refreshed their juice cups with a glass carafe.

"Any ghost stories?" Anne piped, stuffing a bite of egg into her mouth. She still had an uneasy feeling she couldn't shake. She didn't believe in ghosts per se, but it always seemed like the local hotels and inns all had a tale of a haunting or two they were eager to share. Part of the New England charm.

An awkward tinkle of a laugh erupted from Betty. "People believe all sorts of things, especially up around here," she said. "Sometimes, we are too easily influenced by others, don't you think?" She shot Anne a stern look that reminded Anne all too much of her mother.

Anne nodded, sheepish as she chewed. The dark shadows along the bottom of Betty's irises seemed to give a jump and the faint morning light nearly—but didn't fully—cooperate in reflecting against the hard curve of her glasses as Betty topped off their coffees. "Everyone just loves that room. We've had people who've been coming back for years. Something about this place."

As they walked along the harbor to the downtown street with shops and a little boardwalk, Anne's phone buzzed. She ignored it, raising her Canonet Rangefinder instead to take a shot of the bobbing sailboats, their clones resting on a muted, equally cloudy sky in the glassy water. The sky was thick and bloated, threatening to rain at any moment.

"I'm going take some photos, hon, catch up for lunch at the tavern in a bit?" Anne said as they reached the small epicenter of gift stores and candy shops atop a hill over the boardwalk. Sometimes, if she looked at him from a certain angle, he looked like a stranger, even as he smiled at her before taking off toward the bookstore.

The clouds and shadows actually worked well for her black-and-white shots. Anne framed a shot of an arguing couple with a stroller between two old brick buildings, one of which had strutting overhead that cast hard bars of light and shadow. Another of a young woman frowning into a phone in front of an antique store, a beam of light breaking through the clouds just behind her.

Anne was about to snap a shot of an elderly couple on a bench, a small panting dog trapped between them, when something by her ear made her jump.

"Burn."

Anne whirled to see a dazed-eyed older man with a buzz cut and layers of old clothes wavering on his feet.

"*Burned* it," he hissed again. His smell made her nose prickle, and she lowered her camera so he wouldn't grab it as she stepped away.

"I tried!" The man screeched suddenly. A few people's heads turned even as the stream of tourists made a wide circle around them. "But they don't let me. Near. It."

Anne took a step back and then another as the man jabbed his finger toward an ice cream sign on the sidewalk. She quickly turned and ducked into a café, relieved to see the man take off in another direction.

The young barista's eyes followed her up to the counter. "Old Iggy," the girl at the counter said sympathetically. "Ignore him. Sometimes he's nice enough."

An older man swiping through an iPad snorted in disapproval. "His father was a vandal and so was he. Nearly set the damn town on fire."

"I can't *wait* to get out of here," the girl's smile turned longing as she plopped down the coffee. "You from Boston?"

Anne nodded politely and glanced down at her phone, which vibrated insistently. A message from her mother, even though they had just talked yesterday. "You really can't wait any longer," her mother had said then, like she always did, in the same tone she used when she dissuaded Anne from majoring in photography, from moving to New York, from doing anything, really.

Anne had protested feebly. "Massachusetts has the—"

"I know, the highest percentage of old moms." A pause. "You want to be an old mom?"

Now, Anne deleted the message without listening to it and stood at the counter facing the street. Across the way, the toy store's perfectly reflecting window showed a figure with splashes of lighter color marking her face and neck and arms.

The reflection was staring. But of course it was staring at her, if she was staring at it.

She refocused her eyes to see a faint face on the inside of the café window, barely visible. It took her a moment to realize it was herself. It looked like her but *didn't*. It was like a clone, staring at her.

Get it together, Anne, she scolded herself and sipped her coffee, trying to appreciate the caffeine buzz. She'd have to give it up, wine, sushi, all of it, as she let something else take over her body.

You've wasted your life, haven't you?

Anne stood, tossing away the drink. When she stepped outside, she felt something flutter at her shoulder and whirled around, a yelp stifling in her throat as she saw Derick beaming at her, holding something in his hand. A flyer, for a jazz festival tomorrow. "Rain or shine," he said gleefully.

In the bathroom at the tavern, Anne washed her hands in the faux marble sink and glanced at the mirror for a second, herself looking uncertain before she smoothed down her hair and hurried out.

Anne had never experienced insomnia before except the night of her wedding. That night, she closed her eyes and waited, but the heavy, dreamy feeling preceding sleep eluded her as she listened to Derick's gentle snores. When finally she did start to drift off, she jerked awake a second later.

She heard a noise.

She laid perfectly still, her heart pounding, waiting to hear it again. The ghost, she thought wildly, even though she technically did not believe in such a thing.

There it was. A little click. From the foot of the bed.

She sat up, trying to whisper to Derick to wake up, but her throat was parched, and a small squeak came out instead. Then she saw what it was: the minute hand of a wooden clock on the vanity was stuck.

Anne slid into the vanity chair, pushing the clock hand so that it worked again.

Her reflection was barely a silhouette in the darkness with no distinction, no features, a brushstroke of calligraphy ink, nothing really at all.

Anne's fingers ran over the polished wood of the desk, where tiny pockmarks and dents felt like gritty sand. On the desk's single drawer, curled etchings centered around a keyhole.

She tugged the drawer, expecting it to be locked, but found a small red book inside, too thin to be a Bible. "The Science of Dreaming" ran across the binding in faded thin gold script. She opened it to a well-worn crease and could just make out the words from the moonlight that streamed in.

your shadow, or dream, self—the part of you that
sails on during sleep. Reports of "out-of-body"
experiences, doorways to heaven, alien abductions
and angel encounters have all been traced
to separations gone awry between the dream self and
conscious self. A schism can cause unimaginable

She flipped again and the pages settled easily, as if they already knew what they wanted to show her:

Spellcasters used enchanted reflections to communicate
with their dream selves. Properly positioned along
magnetic fields and treated in an ionic formula,
the mirrors let the beholder ask the dream selves
anything they wished.

What a strange book, Anne thought and turned the pages again, to the back of the very last one—

saw too much. The visions drove them to hysterics or
to act on the evil upon evil they believed grew in them.
Some wrote that those not strong enough had been lost,
drawn too far from their bodies into the shadow
realm. One wrote of a dream 'parasite' escapi

The book ended there. Anne turned it back and forth, trying to see the stitching. She wasn't sure if pages had been ripped out, or if there was another volume.

In the mirror, the seams that traced her outline seemed strained, as if her reflection was a one-dimensional dam, holding back a rush of something desperate to seep out. Her eyes blinked, flat like the gaze of a cardboard cutout.

It was the Face again, watching her.

"Are you a ghost?" Anne whispered, even though it was silly. Nevertheless, she still felt clammy, her body tense, ready to run. She whispered even quieter: "A 'dream self'?'"

Shadows moved in sync with the fluttering curtains, where something screeched, distant but high-pitched. A blur moved quickly across the mirror, like wings flapping. She looked closer into the mirror's shadows and could see a world unto a world, a two-storied building with small figures running around it.

"What on earth," Anne whispered and tried to see closer, but the vision faded.

She put the book back in the drawer and stepped back, her heart rocketing like it would shoot her into space. She shook Derick's shoulder, but he grunted, and she took a long, shaky breath.

Nerves. Hormones. She had just gone off her birth control last month and it was messing with her head, obviously. She climbed back into the too-high bed and waited for sunlight

In the morning, Anne squinted at the mirror. She saw herself, looking groggy and perplexed. It was time to test things out in the clarity of the gray morning.

"Hey babe," Anne said casually. "You have a little something on your chin." She motioned to the mirror, but he merely glanced at it, scratched the corner of his beard and adjusted his baseball before stepping away.

"It's weird right?" Anne persisted. She hadn't remembered any of her dreams but slept uneasily. "This place feels a little off."

"Getting more into the ghost stories this trip, aren't you?" He gave her a look as they left the room.

At breakfast, Anne dug into the banana pancakes as Betty set down a ceramic miniature pitcher with maple syrup. "I found a strange book in our room," Anne said. "Is it from a local library?"

Betty smiled blandly. "I'm not sure, we have many books here. The housekeeper cycles them through." She shuffled over to a bookshelf and retrieved a thickly bound book, placing it carefully between them. "That reminds me. If you enjoy your stay do consider us for events."

The book was full of groups posing in the backyard of the inn, mostly wedding parties. A few portraits caught her eye—Anne leaned closer to see one bride, during preparations and in her wedding gown. Anne recognized the same lost look in the stranger's eyes that she felt. On the opposite page was a magnificent full portrait of the couple with "1 Year Anniversary!!!!!!" scrawled beneath it. Anne leaned closer. The bride's eyes looked completely different—self-assured, calm as a cat, with something…sinister about them.

"We've had weddings here, reunions, all kinds of things," Betty grinned. "Think about it."

Outside in the drizzling day, Anne roamed the sprawling hill of the inn's yard with her camera while she waited for Derick to grab an umbrella. At the base of the hill, a lofty white trellis framed a pond. Around that, small fountains and streams fed into each other, surrounded by statues of chipped alabaster deer and frogs.

Half a dozen mirrors, some dirty, were propped up along the fountain streams and behind a birdbath and against trees. Tiny seashells studded along the border of one mirror, with globs of glue in spots. Another was encircled by tiny, rusted figures of monkeys holding coconuts. The rest were unadorned, blank slabs of smudged reflections.

More feng shui, Anne thought. Mirrors were supposed to deflect bad energy, after all.

"Babe!" Derick waved to her, and they headed downtown.

After lunch, Anne explored the many stores while Derick headed back for a nap before the evening's festival. She felt stranger each time she glimpsed her face in store display reflections. It looked more and more like the Face, or like she was forgetting her own features.

A weird mental illness, she thought. *Early Alzheimer's.*

Finally she found what she had been looking for. Iggy dozed next to the door of a gas station a block from the main street, in the same clothes she had seen him in yesterday. A smattering of rain came down as she approached him. Faces inside the gas station turned and moved.

"Burn what," Anne said, and then louder, "*What?* You're talking about the inn, aren't you?"

His eyes glazed, he looked at her for a long moment. When he slowly nodded, an unexpected relief shot through her. It wasn't just her. There was something wrong.

Anne, you are agreeing with a crazy person.

"Is it..." she swallowed her pinprick of embarrassment at the word. "Haunted?"

Iggy gave a half laugh-half cough and closed his eyes.

"I read—or dreamt—something about shadow selves," she whispered. "I think I'm seeing mine. What do I ask it? A wish?" She laughed, it was all so absurd, and yet she knew she was seeing something strange, something had been opened to her and she had to see it through.

Iggy didn't open his eyes or speak, but his head fell forward, and hand opened. In it were five books of matches from the local fusion restaurant with a bright yellow illustration of a parrot. One fell to the ground. She took another from his hand and walked rapidly away.

"Ready for some jazzin'?" Derick asked that evening as he came out of the bathroom.

Anne cleared her throat and shuffled to the vanity. "Check out this book I came across, isn't it—" she opened the drawer, to see "The Science of Dreaming" was gone.

Don't look don't look don't look

Anne glanced at the mirror. Her reflection, the Face, nodded. Her shadow self, she thought. It was right there, waiting for her to ask whatever she wished. *Now,* its eyes seemed to say.

"I'll stay here," she heard herself say, tearing away her gaze to look at him. "I didn't sleep a wink. You go."

After a few minutes of back and forth, Derick agreed. She waited until the door clicked shut and his footsteps disappeared down the hallway before standing at the window, watching him recede. One of the angled mirrors in the yard glinted, even in the dimming sunlight.

The mirrors weren't deflecting negative energy away, she thought and felt a dread creep over her. They were channeling it in.

Burn it, Iggy's urgency came back to her, and she glanced at the lace curtain. She pulled the bright yellow matchbook from her pocket, the logoed Parrot staring up open-mouthed at her.

It would be so easy. But she stopped herself, her pit of unease swelling, and a sharp thought pierced her. What? Burn a place down because she felt a little off? That was *absurd*.

She struck the candle next to the clock instead. Smoke poured from the wick and her nose prickled at the unusual, salt-water smell.

Anne looked up and her shoulders were bare, her reflection naked. Astonished, her hands touched the fabric of the cardigan that lined her collarbone, watching reflected fingers touch skin.

Her shadow self stared back at her just as curiously, and she sensed a crippled, twisted thing behind the veneer of her face.

"Tell me," Anne whispered and felt silly again but then not. "Tell me how to do what I want."

But what did she want?

"I want to be free," she choked.

Darkness crept across her reflection like slowly spreading ink. Anne wiped at her forehead and hair to get it away, slowly at first and then more frantically.

She heard the words form, and imagined they were spoken in the same voice who wrote "The Science of Dreaming."

The shadow self does not care. The shadow self does not compromise.

It was her own mouth, speaking the words in the mirror.

Time drummed, cracked and stopped.

The Face widened its lips and bared its teeth in a mockery of her smile. Something flapped and landed on her head. A flash like scales in water as chains coiled up from her reflection's mouth along her cheeks. The chains gleamed and dripped like sausage casings. And when Anne's eyes moved up to what held the chains—

Anne moaned. The *thing*. It looked like a gargoyle or monkey, a small creature squatting on her head, with a long, lean jaw and tiny pinpricks of eyes full of an all-too-human spite.

The creature shot her a sidelong grin, goo oozing from its mouth as it gave a jerk of the chains through hooked claws and her reflection's head turned in response. Her reflection smiled, as much as it could with its mouth full of chains, like a horse with a bit.

Anne couldn't scream—her throat had collapsed. She wanted to jerk back, knock over the chair, and climb out the window to get away from it, that thing. But she couldn't move.

This is what you wanted to see. While you did nothing there, we've been very busy here.

"Don't show me this!" Anne shrieked, but it came out in a haggard whisper. Her hands frantically patted the top of her hair. Nothing. In her reflection, the hands reached up and caressed the creature.

"What is on my head?" she whispered. She was frozen, the fear short-circuiting any rational thoughts.

A pet. You bred it yourself, in the dark. Feeding it every compromise, every bit of denial. Aren't you proud?

Her hands were trembling, clutched in her lap but stayed uplifted in the mirror. The creature dropped the chains and became a blur in the background as it flew away, the sound of its leathery wings beating against each other, filling the room.

Everyone has them. Little fears. Little denials. But not everyone lets them get so big.

The Face's eyes were completely dark, brimming over with ink as it smiled and leaned forward. Its mouth, now empty of the chains, formed an "o" and tilted down. The candle's flame went out with a soft *pssf,* leaving them in complete darkness.

Anne felt a rush of hot air and couldn't move. *Asleep, a dream of course,* she started to think until the darkness cleared to a monochrome landscape with a gray building straight ahead and more in the far distance. It was, she thought, the inn, the town, the world—in a horrible gray scale.

In front of her, figures paced like people, but *they had no faces—* instead of eyes and noses and mouths there were blurs like smeared charcoal. But the hideous creatures that rode on their backs were sharp and in focus, their knobby legs twisting like bone ridges against the shadow people's backs, their arms wound around necks or flicked chains as if directing disobedient horses whenever the figures strayed too far from the building.

Anne squinted as one figure came closer and saw the smear of a face morph into something recognizable, but only for an instant: It was Betty, the whites of her eyes rolling around, the winged creature on her shoulders with both its gnarled clawed hands stretched into her mouth, turning her head sharply back to the building.

On the ground, other creatures—not even creatures, but masses of dark sinews and gleaming tendons—pulled their way over the dust. One rose up near her feet and turned toward her. Through its dripping, slimed mass, she recognized the Face. Her face.

It spoke with a sympathy that made Anne's heart ache. *I'll do all the things you want. You don't have to struggle.* It flowed up and a gaping hole widened in a muted screech.

Anne recoiled and tried to scream but it launched forward, its hole of a mouth aiming right toward her.

The hot dry air churned into Anne's throat and around her, blotting out the landscape until she was facing her reflection again, gasping for breath and gripping the sides of the chair.

Everything looked different, flatter. Her tension slipped away, like bags of sand cut from her back. She tried to remember what she had been worried about.

The door clicked suddenly. "It's raining way too hard—" Derick said, and light flooded the room. "What are you doing in the dark?"

She turned from the mirror to her husband. She couldn't feel her face. *My shadow self took it*, she thought dully. She couldn't feel anything.

She watched her shadow self say *I don't think it's going to work out. I need to focus on my art. You're a boring distraction.* Her hand, lifting, to take off the wedding band. Anne watched her hand move over *there* but felt it move *here*, effortlessly, as if it were being lifted by invisible threads. She tried to turn to look more clearly at it, but everything was heavy, muffled, much too hard.

She heard the voices rise, watched her hand fling out the ring in an arc of prismatic glinting.

A huge face filled the mirror, showing all its teeth. A moment later, once the light was snuffed out, Anne realized the face was her face.

A door closed and everything went dark. Anne was stuck. She tried to move, to strain and see the landscape around her, to will the blacks into grays. But the thing on her head stirred and she felt heavier than was even possible.

At times, she saw glimpses: her outside self, the dream self, occasionally passed by window displays, puddles, things that made the air shimmer slightly around Anne and strange, gray-ish things come into distorted view: the toy store, an antique store, but only for an instant. Anne tried to jerk toward them but couldn't move.

Not until sometime later, when the gray landscape and building materialized and she could walk, a little bit. *My self is asleep*, Anne realized thickly through her haze. She tried to run away but her creature was large and fierce and didn't give her an inch of slack.

But it was easier now, Anne thought. She was free from decisions, from guilt, from stifled wanting. For the first time, she didn't have to feel *unhappy*.

Ivy bloomed around her, made of darkness, as soft wings beat overhead. She felt something rest gently against her neck. Her mouth full and muffled, she relaxed into the shadows.

FROM SEA TO SHINING SEA

THROUGH THE BLINDS, shadows of roller coasters and broken rides hung suspended in the gloom. The noxious gray sands of Coney Island stretched past the defunct park and, beyond that, Maria could just make out the gleam of purple blobs in the ocean. For a second it looked like an illusion, a trick of the mist bending what little light made it through, and not the bodies of thousands of sea creatures teeming in the water.

"Let's go quick." Roger appeared next to Maria, solemn in his rubber overalls and gloves. "The rain's on the way and won't stop for a week."

They placed the air filters over their faces and headed out, dragging coolers over the sand, trying not to slip on the deflated orbs of jellyfish. The purple *Galactinos*, dubbed "saucers," had appeared a year ago, one of countless new species. Among the amethyst-colored ruins, a few flavorful *Cassiopea omegosa*, "clear bells," had washed up.

"Stinks more than normal," Maria said over her filter.

Roger's eyes crinkled as he grinned. "Half hour max to fill 'em up. Then we're set for a week. I dare you to find an easier paycheck. Those other boats go and haul and spend all their time sorting. They don't know that timing is—"

"Everything. Yeah, yeah," Maria said. The taste of brine slithered its way to the back of her throat despite her filter. "No one geeks out over jellies quite like you."

Acidic clouds rolled over the horizon as they stepped out onto the dock. A film of bubbles glinted on the darkly brewing Atlantic. The blooms had stayed, killing off thousands of fish as warmer temperatures had brought out jellies never before charted.

"Times of day, week, month and year." Roger punched his code into one of the ancient consoles on the dock. The gears beneath it shuddered to life. "Clear bells swim with the saucers and get close to the shore in the morning. No need to rent a boat."

The salt-encrusted rope slid, lifting a submerged bucket. Tendrils hung out of the bucket like bedraggled hair, flicking into the air.

"Ready," Roger said as he steadied the bucket above their coolers.

Maria plunged her rubber gloves into the pile. A few jellies slid off, plopping back into the water with a quiet gulp. She rooted among the quivering bodies, tossing out the purple saucers. She threw out a few spoiled clear bells too—some of them ruined from exposure to *galactinos'* neurotoxins, which the creatures released when stressed.

"I still can't see how people pay a whole buck for a jelly roll," Maria said.

"The salad's actually my best seller. Healthy, fills you up, cheap." Roger turned the crank and the bucket tipped, pouring their haul into the cooler. "Add some soy sauce and vinegar, *delectable*. And don't forget the deep-fried pops."

Maria wrinkled her nose. After they filled the coolers, they'd head back to his place and prep the jellies, remove the tentacles, desalt and transport them to his food stand. She pulled up her hood and visor so she wouldn't feel the burn of the raindrops that started, staccato, on the wood around them.

"Aw, crap. Let's do this last one and head back before it screws up our yield." Roger lowered the bucket back into the water.

Maria plunged her hand into the new batch, wrapping around a particularly large *galactinos* that sat on top of the heap, neatly covering the rest. It seemed to resist as she picked it up, its tendrils whipping toward her face. An unusually large tendril, silver, curled delicately within the center of its purple mass.

"What is *that*?" Maria said. Before she could take a closer look, tentacles wrapped around her arm, squeezing like an unwanted date's grip. She held the purple saucer away from her body. "Uh, Roger?"

"Throw it back," he said as the wind hissed up the beach and sent the bucket creaking. He gripped the bucket with both hands as tendrils lashed at his elbow.

Maria tried to toss the jelly, but its silver tentacle wound tight around her arm, now more like a snake. A jolt ran up the inside of the rubber glove to her shoulder.

"Ow!"

A word, whispered, came to her through the buzz of pain:

Jump.

The dock and sky tilted in Maria's vision, and something flowed over her.

Water.

It was too late to scream. The ocean water rushed into her ears and flooded her suit. She kicked into a crowd of jellies, trying to reach up but the purple saucer pinned her arm. Tentacles wrenched off her filter and pushed into her nostrils.

Words materialized, clear as a voice in her ear:

No. More.

She kicked harder. She wouldn't be buried in this watery grave. More tentacles wound around her and the buzzing in her head intensified, solidifying into a phrase.

No more.

The jellies were…*talking*, somehow. The realization sent a cold shock through her. More inklings bubbled up in her ears while the neurotoxins spanned out in a cloud of purple glitter around her. Her heartbeat quickened too fast, and she tasted something metallic as her vision clouded.

The cloud amalgamated into foggy scenes, tinged in purple.

Sailors collapsing, children coughing, the air thick with acidic discharge.

Poison. Breed. Control.

"*Maria!*" Roger's hands found hers and the water fell away as she slammed onto the dock. She blinked past the lavender haze to see him over her, tearing off the jellies.

She was still drowning under the alarm signals her nerves gave off. Tingles flared across her body where the jellies still clung, their tentacles shooting pulses through her skin.

No more. Our time.

Ours.

She couldn't talk, couldn't see. Her heart hiccuped as a flood of visions swelled.

Poisoned water, toppled ships, flooded cities. Death.

And a purple sea gleaming like a jewel, as far as the eye could see.

BLESSED

THE BULLETS WHIZZED AROUND CARLA, sending up sharp puffs of decimated corn stalks in the fields. She ran a hand over her enlarged belly.

"Get down!" A voice yelled from the stalks.

Carla ignored it and swayed instead, a little dance to soothe her unborn. Fate, and a higher power, would protect her, as she believed all her life it would.

Even when everyone had said something was wrong with her.

Even when everyone had said she hadn't prayed enough, hadn't *wanted* it enough. But she had wanted to carry life, more than anything. She had tried everything the commune members suggested, from sucking down putrid tea to letting the commune leader try and try again to create life in her.

Funny, Carla mused, that she hadn't been gifted with life until she was faced with so much death.

"Get down!" the voice screamed again.

Next to Carla, something dropped.

A head.

The head rolled a few feet away, severed, its hair neatly braided.

The body's neck stump smoked. The weapons in the sky were effective, targeting people like mosquitos in a zapper.

Four people huffed and ran through the corn, louder than laboring cows.

"No! *Miriam*," A bloodstained, petite woman wailed and choked up when she spotted the head.

"We can't stay," a tall woman said. Her intense gaze shot up overheard. "They're here."

The two men with them nodded urgently.

Carla closed her eyes. She was protected by holiness—she didn't need to run.

"Hey. Listen." The tall woman grabbed Carla's hands. "I'm Angelica. The invasion is here, now. We're losing. We have to get out of their line of sight before we end up like…"

"Don't bother," one of the men said. "She's in shock. She'll just slow us down. Knocked up too."

"No, we protect our own," Angelica said, and the words rang familiar. It was like something Carla's commune leader would say when he was still alive. It felt like a lifetime ago that Carla had heard his daily speeches, even though it was just a few days since the invasion, since the commune had caught on fire.

A passing asteroid, the Internet and news sources had claimed when the strange fires started. Turned out to be something else. Some*things* that evaded detection, but while raining fire and noise down from the sky, harnessing lightning itself to split people in two. Carla had witnessed it with her own eyes. Their commune leader had beseeched the otherworldly visitors from his wooden stage, right before a bolt cast his screaming figure into blue and purple flames.

While the other commune members ran in a panic, an overwhelming awe hit her, along with a relief so great she had sunk to her knees. Never again would she need to feel the leader's fingernails, always immaculate and long, raking over her bare shoulders. Never again would she have to feel the dread blanket her as she faced his door.

The Internet called them *Invaders*.

"The Invaders are on us," one of the men said now and grabbed Carla's arm. He dragged her through the corn field. "We can take cover in the barn."

"If we can get out of their line of sight, we might make it!" Angelica said while they ran.

Carla cradled her stomach and half-jogged, best she could, with the others. They didn't understand what it was to be an expectant mother. She wasn't that mobile, invasion or not.

The bloodstained woman moved ahead of them, occasionally shooting a spray of bullets upwards when shadows moved through the clouds. The bullets were too loud, far too loud, but got lost in the hum of the ship overhead.

The humming had started along with the invasion, a sound like motors whirling high above them. At first it had reminded Carla of a giant cicada. Now, she didn't mind the sound anymore. The Invaders, whatever they were, had freed her from the commune, freed her to raise her baby as she wished.

They made it to the barn on the edge of the commune and barricaded the door before introductions. The ones named Omar and Kil investigated the corners of the building for gaps. It almost made Carla laugh. Surely the Invaders could easily get in if they wanted. Omar pulled out a little electronic device. A radio with a cassette player, Carla recognized. Her dad had had one in a box of his old stuff.

"The Invaders don't seem to like certain sounds," Angelica explained. "Recorded music acts as a barrier. Weird, I know, but it's something. Can you tell me about this area? Any food, weapons?"

"There's no food," Carla said at last. "It all burned in one of the falling stars."

"How did you survive?"

"Blessed," she said. "Blessed to carry life, blessed to survive."

A beat of silence from the others, the cassette player wailing pop music, forbidden in the commune. The Invaders' droning sound had receded, and they all seemed to relax a notch.

"God, these religious types," the bloodstained woman, Talee, said, and shot Carla a look like she was week-old meat. Carla wouldn't let it bother her. Just because they didn't give themselves over to a higher cause, others thought they were better. Smarter.

"Faith is about total belief. If you do that, nothing else matters," Carla tried to explain but her words weren't as slick as the leader's had been. They rolled their eyes, but she wouldn't let it bother her.

"Nothing really matters if we're the last of mankind," Kil said. He hadn't stopped trembling since they got to the barn.

"Humankind," Omar corrected. He had a glazed look like some of the commune members when the invaders first arrived. Shock, Carla supposed.

"What do you think they want?" Kil asked.

"Who knows," Talee said. "Water? Food? The planet for themselves?"

"Maybe they'll see how bad we screwed it up and change their minds."

"You hear how some people are changing? Like *metamorphosizing...*"

Carla tuned out the conversation, perching on a pile of rotting wood and rubbing her uterus in the unconscious motion that had become habit.

"How far along are you?" Angelica crouched next to her with a sad smile.

"Just a few days."

"A few..." Angelica looked at Carla's belly and took a step back, uncertainty stitched across her brow.

"I told you I was blessed," Carla said.

"Heads up!" Kil yelled. Outside, the droning intensified to a chainsaw-like pitch, loud enough to blow the doors clear off the barn.

"They protect their own," Carla explained over the noise. The day the reports came in about the asteroid was when Carla prayed harder than she ever had before. When the commune leader had fallen asleep, she had snuck a look at his computer to read frantic internet forum musings about aliens taking people for experiments.

"You can take me," she had said out her open window that night. *"If you let me have my own baby."*

"My own" was an important part of her wish. The commune took most of the newborns to the older women for childrearing. Her plan had always been to leave as soon as she was pregnant. To raise the child as her own.

The next morning, Carla had woken up to all the signs of pregnancy: her stomach ballooned up, tiny kicks like twitches from under her belly. The Invaders had heard her prayers. Accepted her and whoever else might have offered themselves up as vessels.

A true commune, she had thought that morning, praying in tearful joy.

"Carla! Come here!" Angelica motioned frantically from where she and the others crouched behind a pile of hay on the other side of the barn. Instead, Carla rubbed her belly while she headed toward the door.

To the cassette-player.

"Don't touch it!" Omar hollered and raced toward her.

"They need to come in," Carla said. She sensed it just as she sensed the life within her, waiting. It was time to—what did they call that maternal instinct—*nest*. The Invaders needed to get everything ready for the next stage of their takeover, just as she needed to prepare for her child's birth. Her soon-to-be mother's intuition told her there were others like her across the globe, select humans that had given their bodies to usher in a new world. A world with the Invaders as their fathers, midwives, mentors. Carla shivered in excitement at the thought.

She leaned down for the device. The Invaders moved behind the barn door, starbursts of light breaking in through the cracks in the wood.

Ready for her.

Omar nearly reached her before she pressed the stop button. The doors flew open and dazzling lights in a color she couldn't define shot out, muting the others' screams.

The Invaders floated into the barn, too bright to look at directly. They loomed wider and taller than humans, ringed by prismatic flashes that pulsed in hums in a language not yet known to her.

Like they're made of star beams, Carla thought dreamily.

One creature reached to her with the semblance of a hand. The finger-like appendages burned gently when she clasped them.

Their cool fire swept the other humans, leaving her unharmed. The baby turned inside her, eager.

She had known all along.

She was blessed.

THE CIRCUS KING

THE CIRCUS KING slid into her customary grin as the first guests shuffled into the tent. She lifted the scepter that lay next to her—occasionally it took the form of a whip, or a long staff—and greeted families from atop her perch.

"Gather gals and ghouls! Feast on fantastic feats of fascination... astounding aerial acrobatics...dazzling and delightful dancers...Clever and capricious clowns!" The Circus King said, her voice rich in a decades-old smoker's baritone. The Circus King's words fell with little effort. Sometimes she tried to form other words. "*Where am I*," or "*help*," but only shrill declarations of the show would manifest.

Peanut shells and popcorn kernels crunched under the guests' feet, like so many casings of a swarm of insects that had hatched all at once.

The Circus didn't sell peanuts.

It didn't sell anything.

And yet, the tickets and the peanuts and the candy and cups of soda all appeared.

A single yellow light fell on the Circus King, a perfect concentric outline on her perch next to the stage. A little girl with a blue candy-stained mouth gaped up at her, until the Circus King widened her smile, so large until it seemed she would swallow up the whole tent. For this performance, Circus King took the shape of a round man with a shelf-like nose, a mustache worthy of a twirl, and tufts of orange hair. Her crown had taken the form of a towering hat.

"Delight in devilish dances! Leer at lunging leapers…juggling jesters…mega merrymakers! Indulge in ingénues incredible!"

A wisp of nighttime air, warm and salty, swirled in with the visitors from the open flap in the tent. The Circus King sometimes tried to look out through the entrance from her perch, but her thoughts would grow murky. The Circus' way of saying *no*. Whether it was the tenth or hundredth performance, the Circus King couldn't remember. Time blurred in the tent, smudged beneath the shadows of the guests.

"Ready, rousing rascals? Revel, relish, and reel…see sights so staggering…frolic in the festivity of fools and fiends!"

As soon as the last person sat in the last seat, the show began. Clowns flew out from their hiding spots, too small or too large or too round to be real humans. The audience cheered as one beat another with an oversized mallet, other clowns egging on the violence. Pink and blue blood splattered out of the beaten clown, who grabbed its rainbow entrails and screeched.

Another performer, large as an ape and with a crimson face, knocked over the group.

The audience laughed harder.

The Circus hummed, pleased.

The Circus King didn't know much, only that the Circus wanted this. The more she could coax the audience to give into their frenetic energy, the better the creatures performed.

The show continued, with acrobats flicking across the ring like larger-than-life crickets. The Circus King imagined stunts and the performers executed them, as if someone had scraped out a window to her mind and all the creatures could catch a glimpse. Though the costumes and colors changed, her show stayed the same.

Except for tonight.

A new, green-tinged creature wove between the jugglers tossing sticks of fire. The trickster bumped into one of the jugglers' knees and fell over.

Some of the audience laughed, thinking it was a routine. But it wasn't routine; it was a wrinkle in her otherwise flawless show.

The Circus King refocused past her irritation and continued to shout.

"Prepare for perplexing possibilities! The fantastic fiery finale! Dazzling, delirious, and death-defying!"

The green trickster leapt and gestured, trying to get the viewers' attention, but all of their eyes fixed on the grand finale: dancers leaping through rainbow-colored rings of fire that descended from the ceiling. The Circus King reveled in their applause, in the Circus' approval.

Once the last of the audience had left, the music and light dissipated. The tent shrunk and sealed itself shut. Usually after a performance, the creatures climbed and clung to one another in a pile of flesh, some fornicating in the shadows. The Circus King would doze above on her perch, limbs heavy, as they all waited in a drowsy twilight. When the time came to perform again, the Circus would alert her, the lights would come back on.

But this time, something was amiss.

"Hyucka Hyucka Hyucka!" Some of the clowns made the facsimile of a laugh during the performance and continued it now as they ran in a circle along with other creatures, unseeing eyes bright as plastic.

The Circus King leapt down from her perch and snapped her scepter against the ground. The creatures ignored it. She moved them aside, their bulbous flesh yielding to her scepter. They circled a blot marring the ground.

"What is this?" The Circus King murmured.

A hole, about the size of a fist. The floor of the Circus varied—this time it appeared as cracked wood, strewn with hay and peanuts and the droppings of some animal.

She circled the hole. Her crown throbbed at her head, heavy enough to snap her neck in two.

The creatures paused. Not quite turned toward her and not quite toward the hole either. One of the clown's mouths looked like a gash that needed sewing. The Circus King didn't know what any of them were made of, only that she had once seen this clown bend over, its buttons strained and popped to reveal nothing but darkness beneath the streaked polka dots. Next to it, the new greenish trickster, tinier than the rest, watched her intently.

She turned back to studying the hole. No draft came from it, only a peculiar smell that she couldn't quite place but made her uneasy, that lifted a small crack in the back of her mind, a bend at the baseboard of the few thoughts she could manage.

Another one of the Circus' many tricks. The Circus King couldn't bring herself to get closer to peer down the hole. They were in the Circus' belly and whatever sat at its core lay in that darkness. Something about it felt ravenous, foreboding.

Maybe tomorrow it would go away.

As the Circus King dozed and waited for the next show, snatches of memories came back to her, unleashed from their cage, as if the hole in the ground had prompted an opening in her mind.

She remembered pigtails against her ears and sugar-crusted lips. She had been with her father. *Pa.* A great longing swept her, past the feeling of a cotton candy stick, wisps curling against her sticky fingers. The sun sinking low behind them had cast ribbons of shadow and light on the water beyond the pier. Pa's grimy nails pressed into a black-and-white flyer.

"It'll be fun."

Evelyn, that was her name, it came to her now and again—Evelyn remembered the dread she had felt when she and her father turned away from the boardwalk, away from the crowds, and down an alleyway in the tiny coastal town. They and a few others headed toward the circus, set far back from the pier.

"It'll be fun," Pa kept saying. "Maybe we'll see the world's smallest man or acrobats."

The tent loomed in great red and white stripes, shining with newness. The first few drops of rain flicked off its surface as though the Circus lived under its own force field. It whispered, its stripes shuddering in the wind.

Evelyn had stopped. She didn't want to go into the tent. She dropped the cup of soda. Her dress was a mess. Pa's brow darkened, telling her to be more careful. It was her nice dress, ruined. She didn't care, didn't even like the dress. He gave her a warning slap on the arm, the jolt sending her cotton candy flying to the ground. She watched in horror as the delicate pink candy darkened next to her shoes.

She cried but Pa chided her again before turning on his heel and marching toward the tent, leaving her to follow.

The tent ahead of her flapped as if to get her attention but she looked down at her ruined treat, raindrops catching in her lashes as she wished with all her might that she would never see Pa again. Wisps of the cotton candy against the damp bricks morphed, spreading into wings. Hardened nubs of the candy lengthened like a spine, as fluffs of pink expanded and enveloped her.

Evelyn had emerged, stretching and straining in the Circus' spotlight on her perch, speaking her ringmaster lines as if in a dream. It was where she had been ever since.

Evelyn shuddered the inchoate mass of sensation and memory away. Her fingers—far too long—flapped like banners against her moist cheeks. The crown, like wrought iron, seared into her scalp.

She was the Circus King now.

Nevertheless, she remembered. Her plastic shoes full of pebbles. Strands of cotton candy hardening into pink commas against the bricks in the rain. Her palms, streaked and empty.

The next night, the hole had grown five feet at least. The creatures performed dutifully around it, but the Circus King had other problems. The unwelcome trickster had returned, ruining her show.

"See succulent and surreal sights!" The Circus King shouted to the rapt audience. "Sassy simpletons soaring sublimely!"

The green trickster marched up to the audience between the sword-swallowing act and the contortionist. The trickster stuck one foot in the air and jumped up like a cannonball, leaving a trail of green and blue feathers in its wake.

"Disbelieve daring deeds!" The Circus King continued. "Prepare your popping peepers..."

The trickster continued to spin in the air like a sick bird as visitors clapped and strained to grab the feathers. A completely new performance that the Circus King had no control over.

"...for the fantastical fiery finale!"

That evening, the Circus had transformed Evelyn into someone with more girth than she was used to. Her belly swelled under satin fabric, and she wore a hat that seemed to reach halfway up to the tent. She barked the laugh of an old man about to reveal a wicked secret.

The end couldn't come fast enough. After the crowd left, the Circus King leapt down, using her prop—now a jewel-studded staff—to push the performers aside. Half a dozen dancers shimmered in their outfits like nighttime beetles. The clowns with their painted grins turned toward her, grimly attentive. She resisted stepping back. She would not retreat; she was the Circus King.

"What do you want?" she said to the hole, and the creatures.

As usual, the clowns didn't react, aside from the occasional "hyucka." Their eyes bore into her, white and matte, no more effective than pasted squares of paper. They watched with something else, smell or sound or another sense the Circus King was unaware of.

The hole gaped in the center as Evelyn neared its edge. Its inkiness suggested an unthinkable depth, stretching to the other side of the planet and beyond. A hint of something else wafted in that vastness, something not of this world. It was the same presence that had grown the Circus and its performers in a monstrous shell, with Evelyn at its center like a pearl.

Everything in her wanted to run from that hole. But she thought of her pa, the ocean breeze. She marched to the edge of the tent to stab the fabric with her staff. No way through. She swung around and smacked her staff against the nearest clown. It soared a few feet as if it were made of stuffed pillows. It landed with neon blue splatter and a giggle.

"I'll smash them all," Evelyn said between breaths. "If you don't let me out."

The trickster emerged from the group. Unlike the others, its eyes were cold, calculating.

Seeing.

It gestured to itself emphatically, as if to say *mine.* The creature was small, with bulging cheeks and hair like yarn. It glared at her with eyes all too human—resentful and full of rage.

It gestured again. *Mine.*

"You wished too. To be here," The Circus King said, and her baritone had vanished, a higher squeak of a voice returning. *Evelyn's* voice. "Well, it was a mistake. A trick. You can have this horrible circus. I'll leave."

Evelyn jumped when she saw her hands—still far too long but thinner, smoother, than she had seen in a long time. Her own oval nails hovered beneath the shadows that steamed over her skin. The tight band around her temples flared. She tried to yank off the crown, but it felt embedded on her head.

One of the performers spoke. A smaller clown, with a painted orange smile. "Hyucka. Only one king." Its words were thick and squished like mud splatters. It sounded like a pile of worms that had joined together to try to mimic human speech.

"One," the clown managed again. It lifted its white hands, bulky like stitched stubs of fungi-covered sausages. It pointed to the hole. "Waste."

Evelyn understood now. The trickster contended for her crown, to be a new Circus King who could offer fresh visions. But that would mean Evelyn would have to be disposed of.

The trickster neared her, less the size of a child and more Evelyn's own height now. She couldn't tell if she was shrinking or it was growing.

"Whatever happened to you, the Circus doesn't make it better," Evelyn said. "But you can have this crown. Here." She tried again to wretch off the crown, but it held steady, branded into her skin. "Let me leave!"

She saw no way out; all the openings were sealed aside from the terrible pit. She'd rather be Circus King forever than face that unnatural darkness. The pit wasn't freedom. It was worse than death, that much was clear, clear as the growing impatience that emanated from it. She would be cast out, far from this Earth, into the bowels of some region from which she could never return.

Evelyn tried not to shriek as the performers stepped closer, locking her and the trickster around the hole. It was simple to them. One Circus King stayed, one Circus King left.

The Circus breathed, waiting.

The trickster, the child, whatever it was, had crept too close, its sharp hands closing on Evelyn's wrists as it tried to yank her into the hole. Evelyn raised her staff, but it deflated like a half-filled balloon. She dropped the staff and kicked the trickster square in its belly. It squealed but held on.

The performers around them shifted, giving them space while they struggled. The pit seemed darker, eager to be filled, to flush out its waste.

Evelyn's ringmaster boots scraped closer to the hole.

"No," she cried, and the trickster's white teeth glinted.

Evelyn remembered the heavy reassurance of her pa's hand, wisps of candy dissolving on her tongue mixed in with the scent of ocean air after sunset.

There could only be one Circus King. But there *had* to be one.

Evelyn gritted her teeth and changed her grip to take hold of the trickster's arms. It realized too late what she planned as Evelyn propelled both of them forward.

There *had* to be one.

They plummeted down the hole. The trickster shrieked as Evelyn kicked in the darkness. Her hair grew thin and long and short, her body stretched and shrank and collapsed and expanded.

The sensation of falling stopped. Evelyn floated in the emptiness, the trickster's panicked breathing behind her.

"I'll bring them all down here. Every single one of your contenders," Evelyn said, her words immediately swallowed by the pit. "So you will never have a Circus King."

A pressure bore into her skin on all sides and the crown prickled around her head. She touched her forehead, finally freed and scraped raw by the clamp. The darkness flickered like curtains separating, yielding to a softer blackness and her face opened, spreading like the unfolding of a cape.

The trickster floated in front of her, the metal ring clamping around its greenish skin. It grinned at her before it grew, stretching into the Circus King.

They were both were expelled out in a great rush of wind.

Evelyn stood outside, her mind as empty as the icy, ink-stained sky above. She ran her tongue over crushed sugar cubes and burnt kernels, looking for Pa on the boardwalk.

Something was wrong—her clothes didn't fit right, and her hair seemed like someone else's, brushing past her shoulders and out of their pigtails. Her feet ached, too big for her shoes. She had grown taller it seemed, as though she had missed a birthday or two.

Circus music started up nearby, sending a bolt of panic through Evelyn's muddied thoughts. Though her heart hammered and every inch of her told her to run, it seemed important—very important— that she walk slowly, away from the droning music and toward the water, where the moonlight on the waves flickered like a warning. She didn't want to draw the attention of what felt like a massive creature lying just out of reach, resting.

Maybe someone could help her find Pa.

Behind her, the Circus played on.

PUDDLE OF COMRADELY DESPAIR

WHEN I CAME TO, I was a collapsed pile of half-liquified bones in the middle of 148th street. Literally. No shit. Just lying there like an egg frying in a bored kid's driveway.

"Could you help me out here?" I called to passersby. But it was the city and people barely batted an eye, even if you were a semi-formed skeleton in the middle of Hamilton Heights.

I couldn't remember much—a train screeching, a woman's tear-stained face and a shock like lightning, electrifying every bit of me. And now I was here, my senses somehow intact enough to see the bones that made up my body but unable to move. Lucky me. It stank like day-old trash and urine, gasoline and grease, fried dough and sweet nuts and all the things you definitely don't want to be smelling for hours.

Damned assholes. Not a single person stopped a second to check me out. Figures. Probably thought I was a publicity stunt or busted up animatronic. It took almost 15 minutes before someone paused.

Pause would be generous. The woman, maybe in her twenties, earbuds glowing, barely glanced at me as she waited at the corner for traffic to slow.

"Help me out here?" I asked again, but the woman's face was marble, detachment like a brick wall in her eyes. Whatever I was, she had no time for it. "C'mon?"

"Blow me," she said out of the side of her mouth. I studied her chipped purple painted toenails in their beat-up flip-flops. When the traffic slowed enough, she darted across the street.

I pleaded to the dozens of shoes that passed. Sometime later, purple toenails reappeared.

"You're still here," she said. "Man, this is some elaborate TikTok shit."

"Not a stunt," I said. "Help me out, c'mon."

"What's in it for me?" She dumped a little bag of Skittles in her mouth and chewed loudly, contemplating as people streamed by.

Gradually the answer billowed in, arriving from the ancient magic that ran in the rat-laden cracks and hollow layers beneath the city, the same stuff that somehow powered me to consciousness.

I didn't know how I knew anything at this point. It was all screwy, really, and I didn't know what I was gonna say til I said it.

"I can manage a wish," I said finally. What about that! Like some kind of goddamned genie. I was almost proud. "But nothing too big. Think a grand from a lotto ticket, something like that."

I thought she'd go for the money—why the hell wouldn't she—but her face didn't move.

"I want you to kill someone," she said. "Can you do that?"

I considered, letting the answer form as instinctively as a fly seeks out shit. "Maybe. Who?"

"My landlord. He sucks." Her face darkened for a second.

"I can do that. But you gotta help me."

"What do you need?"

"A body. Yeah, that's it," I said.

She brushed back a strand of hair, a determined jut to her jaw and nodded before picking me up.

The simple agreement was enough that I was able to slide into her sleeves and—no shit—turn into clothes! My femurs fixed onto the back of her legs as skeleton stockings. My head shifted into a beanie painted with a grinning skull matching the tights. My hands settled into her own, a skull bracelet appearing on her wrist. Everything hummed.

"Hell yeah, now we're talking," I said enthusiastically, feeling better than I had in a while. "Yeah, hey, let's go somewhere fun." I had a few ideas in mind but didn't know if she'd be game.

"First, landlord." She walked in that hunched clipped pace that said *screw you* to the world.

"What's your name, by the way?" I asked. I could see a lot up here. I felt almost normal.

"Avery," she said.

"I like that."

"Whatever, man. What's your deal? How'd you get here, I mean," Avery asked, and I struggled to remember.

"No clue. I was…fighting. My ex maybe. In the subway. I think… maybe we both fell."

Avery mused for a second. "The F train was super delayed today. Like, suicide-homicide-level-delayed. Was that you?"

The screech, the honk, the flash of darkness rolled over me, but it was too fuzzy to tell.

"She probably did this to me," I said. Anger was like a flood, darkening my vision. "There was always something weird about her, you know? Too much patchouli. Maybe she's a witch and cursed me."

"You can't just say that, man. Most witches are chill."

"Satanist?" I tried. She rolled her eyes, disgusted at my lack of knowledge, apparently.

"Or maybe you were just a dick, and this is your personal hell," she said.

I nodded, a flash of skeleton print against the black beanie. "Yeah, OK, maybe. That's fair. I'd take this, I guess, over some underground fantasyland. Like a limbo between worlds."

Now that I was thinking about it, I could see other gray forms, ghosts I guess, in the city. Fused on doors and clothes and glass like some sort of half-visible graffiti. They were all blurred, all indistinct, living in their own little worlds.

A purgatory.

For all of us.

The sight of them was giving me the heebie jeebies, so I tried to laugh it off. "Least I don't have to leave the city."

"Whatever man," she said but it was the friendliest she had been.

Her muscles locked up as we got to the chipped, puke-green doorway set within grime-covered rust bricks.

"Why don't you just move?" I asked.

"Nowhere else to go. Mom got this rent controlled, so it's literally impossible for me to move. And now that she's..." Avery stopped, the words dying in her throat.

"So what'd this douche do?" I said as we mounted the dark, narrow staircase. The smells, damn! It was worse than baking on the sidewalk. Pungent sweat and ripe trash, mixed in with someone's overcooked mac-n-cheese.

"Not worth talking about," Avery said, each word snapping like a wad of gum. I could feel the beads of sweat under her hair, the nervous hammering of her heart. Poor kid. I hadn't known her long, but no one deserved this kind of crap.

"Don't you have someone who can help you out, kid? A friend or family?"

She shook her head, a hard glint in her eye. "I don't need anyone." She said it with such vehemence, I believed her.

"You need someone, kid," I said. "Find a nice guy, a friend, something. I know it's hard, believe me. But you can't go it alone in life."

"We're all alone," she snapped. I could feel bad things bubbling up at the edge of her mind, like her brain had eaten a spoiled taco. A memory here, a feeling there, trying to gain a foothold. They started to materialize but she quickly walled them off. Nope, nothing to see here.

"Go ahead to his door," I said.

She hesitated. "He's a lot...bigger."

"I got this. Go on."

She waited another second but then knocked.

I could tell the guy was bad news by the way he loomed in the darkness, like he didn't have a care in the world. It was in his eyes, blue like drained ice, a buzz cut like he had been in the military. His eyes were flat, lizard-like, something mean dancing at the edges that pooled and crystalized when he focused on her.

"Like the look, Avs," the landlord said, his gaze raking up and down her. I had to hand it to her, she repressed a shudder and kept herself still. "Very goth."

"Hey," I said and almost laughed at seeing him jump. His gaze flew up, confused, to her hat.

I winked, the fabric moving as easily as skin.

He stepped back, sun-spotted forehead wrinkling. A strength flowed from me, primordial, like I was a goddamn gorilla. We strode forward, closing the distance in the room that stank like mold and BO.

A feeling flowed into Avery's hands, like a really good buzz, and let me take over. I reached up and choked him. It wasn't hard. His neck squished like hospital Jell-O, cords and tendons popping under her fingers. Her bitten nails dug into his damp neck folds.

He grunted, swinging at us. But his meaty fists bounced off Avery's shoulders as if she was made of tire rubber.

"This is rad," Avery murmured. She smiled.

The landlord locked eyes with me in a fury, even as the dawning of death crept into his features. Fucked up recognizing fucked up. I squeezed, feeling skin, muscle and blood vessels collapse together in a pulpy mass.

Bye asshole.

He heaved one more time and toppled onto the stained rug.

We stared at his still body. The room was quiet. Peaceful even. An AC jammed into a window rattled.

"You're taking this well," I said. She had murdered someone with her bare hands but didn't seem to mind.

"Do we need to wipe our prints or something?" Avery said, still staring.

I reached down and grabbed his Gucci wallet, an obvious Chinatown fake. I pulled out two wrinkled twenties and flipped the wallet onto his chest.

"Nah," I said. The power that had flowed through us filled me with reassurance. She'd be safe from suspicion. And no one would believe someone her size could've taken this scumbag out. "It was your wish. No one's going to trace anything. You're good."

"That was insane!" Avery said once we were back in the hallway. Adrenaline soared through her blood, making me want a cigarette. "I feel like Batman. What do we do now?"

"Let's slow down a sec."

"What's wrong with you?" she asked.

I wasn't feeling too well. The hallway bobbed like a ship. I slid off her, the stockings and hat and bracelet turning back into the pile of bones on the filthy once-red hallway rug.

"Sorry, kid. Looks like it's time for me to go. Maybe this is some penance done or something. Weirder things have happened in the city," I said, but I didn't know what.

Her lip shook a little and I was touched. I had made a friend. No joke, it felt good.

"Hey," I croaked. "Maybe I'll see you again."

I was losing juice and fast. Things wobbled like a phone screen in the rain. My bones started to melt into the rug. I saw other gray creatures, clearer now, watching me, some moaning, trying to tell me something. Warn me? Welcome me?

Whatever it was, I did not want anything to do with that, no thanks. I struggled to stay put, but it didn't seem like I had much choice in the matter. My bones were liquefying in front of my eye sockets.

"Wait!" Avery cried. "Can I have one more wish?"

"Don't know," I managed. "Things aren't looking good, but you can give it a try."

"Can you stay?"

The unsettling feeling of my bones melting stopped for a second. "You sure, kid? I don't really know how this thing works. You could be stuck with me a long time."

"It's kinda nice having someone around," she said, sounding more like the kid she was and not a hardened city vet, like me.

"You really don't mind having me leech onto you?" I asked.

"Nah," she said. "You can stay. I owe you one. And we can do stuff, you know?" That glint in her eye came back and I could hear the locked things rustling in her mind like bats waking up, ready to get out. "Take out pervs in the city. No one will suspect."

A little bit of power flowed back into me, and I could move my jaw again enough to grin. She reached out, grabbing what was left of my metacarpals.

"Kid, I think we're gonna have fun together."

MACABRE ELVES

"THINK tonight'll be the night we see the elves?" I said, dropping down from the chain-link fence onto pine needles and packed dirt. I winced when the landing sent a jolt up my busted arm, then followed Chase between the looming fir trees in the silent, snow-dusted Christmas tree lot.

No one except us and the rats were up at this hour, but we still ducked under the video camera. I smirked at the thought of the camera catching Chase's wrinkled elf outfit and plastic pointed ears. I had opted for jeans and windbreaker, with dots of red face paint slathered on my cheeks and a huge-ass floppy green hat.

"Will tonight be the night?" Chase echoed in a fake announcer's voice, panning the trees with his phone. We stopped under a sagging cardboard photo op of a cartoon mouse decorating a tree. "When the Macabre Elves initiate their newest members on Christmas Eve?"

He turned his phone toward me.

I flipped him the finger.

"Jared has no chill," he went on in his announcer's voice.

"Dude. No real names."

Beyond the lot, our bumfuck town of Nowheresville stretched out. Garlands of lights wrapped around the two- and three-storied houses, blinking in a frenzy even from here. It was the kind of picture-perfect small town that brought in hipster tourists and families from the city in latte-inspired frenzies, eager for selfies on the historic main street, the carolers, the whole shebang. Of course, they didn't see the kids like us, the unlucky ones that every town had. Invisible. The holidays sucked more than anything for us— a reminder of everything we were missing out on.

"The Macabre Elves are awesome, and we want in," Chase continued. The shiner his uncle had given him had finally started to fade, but you could still see a little puff around his eye. "We're in the last spot you guys were sighted. We hope we're worthy. We live to serve."

We were obsessed with joining the Macabre Elves ever since they showed up last month, just before Thanksgiving. No one knew what they wanted. People had spotted the costumed figures at the edge of the mall after hours, at the top of the hill near the train tracks, and in one of the countless Christmas tree lots. The elves were spotted standing, waving, sometimes dancing, sometimes still, but always from a distance.

Normally it'd be the kind of cutesy thing this town would lap up. Except for one fact that showed up again and again in eyewitness accounts and handfuls of low-res pics people had managed to snag.

The Macabre Elves carried big-ass knives.

The newspaper went into a frenzy, giving the group their nickname and writing breathy pieces. Rumors ran like crazy. A gang. Escaped psych ward patients. A whacko circus family. Serial killers. A new band trying to go viral. And no matter how much the police looked, they could never find them. The elves would disappear without a trace. People who had seen them close up acted a little weird after, like they had PTSD or something.

It was freakin' hilarious.

There was another reason we were obsessed: a screen shot from a security camera had captured the face of one of the elves, her pigtails and full-lipped scowl haunting my dreams ever since.

"Think she'll show?" I sucked in a breath of cold air and pine needles.

"Hope so." He offered me a clove cigarette and we settled onto the ground. "Arm hurt?"

"Nah." I supported my braced elbow with my other hand, trying not to think of the latest ambush behind school. My ribs still had the bruises to show for it.

"Screw Stephan," Chase said after a minute.

"Yeah, screw Stephan," I agreed. I envisioned five billion ways to get my revenge on a daily basis, but we didn't stand a chance against Stephan and his meathead friends.

"Post the video?" I lit the cigarette. We hoped the Macabre Elves would see it and let us join their gang, cult, whatever they had going on. It was a long shot but couldn't hurt.

Chase nodded. "Now we wait."

I started to doze off when Chase nudged me an hour later. Four figures stood silhouetted in the moonlight between two trees. I sat up straighter when I noticed the pigtails. We both got to our feet.

"The video worked, dude," he whispered. "Merry Christmas to *us*."

"I feel like we should kneel or something."

"Dude. Be cool." Chase smoothed the ruffled collar of his elf outfit.

The moonlight illuminated their faces while they marched toward us—four bobbing heads painted white, pink, or green, with contrasting lips and eyelids, all with some variation of pointed ears and striped outfits.

I tried not to stare at the pigtailed elf, her face painted light green and lips the color of bile, but I couldn't help it. Her plump curves strained against a red dress and striped leggings. She wore a crooked name tag that read *McMittens*.

I was in love.

McMittens twirled an oversized candy cane in her gloved hands and winked at me. I tried to shoot my coolest smile back.

"Well," the tallest of the elves rasped, her voice like a dog showing its teeth. The ringleader. Her giant burgundy beehive hair strung with colored lights towered over us. The way she held herself made me think of a department store manager. The name tag on her white-and-blank striped bodysuit read *Gingersnap.* "You wanna be one of us, huh?"

"We live to serve," Chase said. I nodded, my eyes falling to the Chef-style kitchen blade tucked into Gingersnap's belt.

"You're in luck then," McMittens piped up. Her voice rang deep, with the same underlying growl that set my skin prickling. Whatever, she was still hot.

The third elf, bent over like a broken tree branch, mimed something with fur-lined gloves, his face leering at us from under pasty pink paint. A matted headband with pointed ears rose from his tangle of black curls and he started slashing the air with a bread knife like a deranged fencer.

"Blitzen approves," McMittens said through her plump green lips, and I grinned at her.

"Jared," I introduced. "And Chase."

"We're ready for the Macabre Elves initiation, whatever that may be," Chase said.

"Yeah." I lit a cigarette to keep my hands steady. "This town sucks. Home sucks. School sucks. We wanna stir some shit up."

"So why do you do it?" Chase asked eagerly. "Why elves? Is that, like a thing?"

"Elves, clowns." Gingersnap shrugged, her beehive wobbling. "Depends on the season. Everyone likes a costume." She uncapped a flask. "You want to join, start with this. It makes what comes next more palatable." Against the night sky, her white-painted face glowed stark against the black rings outlining her eyes and mouth.

"Easy," I said. We'd been working on our alcohol tolerance since grade school. We took turns chugging. Cheap whiskey.

"So, what's your MO? Break-ins? Stalk people?" Chase bounced on the balls of his feet, his fake ears wagging. "Cause we're down for whatever."

Blitzen mimicked a silent laugh from behind Gingersnap, his fake ears like horns in the shadows.

"We're a little more creative," the fourth elf said, his hooked nose looked like it had been broken too many times. Same smoker's voice as the other two. His name tag, covered by red suspenders, looked like it read *Jolly Pants*.

"You join us, you don't have to worry about being pushed around." McMittens widened her smile.

I was about to smile back when I noticed her teeth: completely black.

"Whoa!" I jumped, bumping into Chase.

"Think they're ready?" Gingersnap asked.

"I, ah, I might be good—" I said before Chase nudged me silent. I couldn't tell if they all had funky teeth, but I wasn't ready for any last-minute dental work, even with the alcohol buzzing through my head.

"Sure, sure." Chase tried to hide the pitch of panic in his voice. "What is the next step, exactly?"

The four had lined up in a loose circle around us. I shuffled back, realizing how dumb this was. Chase had slipped on his brass knuckle rings, probably thinking along the same lines as me. McMittens opened her mouth wider, and I swear I could see the headlines online tomorrow – "TEENAGERS EATEN BY CANNIBAL ELVES" – when something like tar wiggled out of her mouth.

The other three elves opened their mouths and rolled their eyes back while they spit out more of the same.

For a second, I thought they were puking, until the blobs of tar dripped from their mouth and congealed to perch on their shoulders. The blobs looked like spiders but longer, bigger, the size of a goddamn Chihuahua.

They were alive.

"F—f—f—" Chase dropped his brass knuckles and couldn't get another sound out.

I tried to suck some air back into my lungs and staggered back.

The creatures writhed on the shoulders of their elves, looking like something you'd pull out of a clogged sink—black and tangled, a mass of tentacles, or tails, or fur.

"What. The. Hell," I managed.

"You want in or no?" Gingersnap's lips moved, eyes still blank. Her voice sounded clearer. "You'll get a new pet. You'll have to feed it every so often with whomever you deem appropriate."

She pulled out two empty shot glasses. The mass on her shoulder, now looking like a spiky sea urchin, moved down to deposit two smaller masses the size of roaches in the glasses.

Baby blobs.

"F-F-Fuck off!" Chase yelled, kneeling and rooting frantically in the dirt for his brass knuckles.

"Nothing can hurt us," McMittens said. Her inkblot creature twirled down along her arm and wrist, over old cigarette burn scars and faded slash marks.

And jumped directly at me.

Chase and I both screamed as McMittens' creature ran over my elbow, sending a shot of ice down my arm, before it jumped back onto her shoulder like a well-trained bird.

The deep ache that had settled into my busted arm vanished.

"What the?" I took off the brace and bent my elbow.

"Back the hell up, freaks." Chase stood, brandishing his brass knuckles.

"Pain is gone," I said.

"For real?" Chase lowered his fist an inch.

"They let you do whatever you want. Go where you want." McMittens' head tilted and, even though her eyes were milky and unfocused, she seemed to be studying me. "You'll have fun. They don't leave a trace."

"Like what, eat people?" My teeth chattered. I thought I saw tiny silver teeth flash in one of the blobs. "Is that what's up with the knives?"

"People…*listen* better when they see a weapon," Gingersnap said. "But we don't need to get our hands dirty. Unless you want to."

"They suck on people's energy," McMittens said dreamily. "Little tastes, here and there. Invisible. Untraceable. They never know what hits them. Maybe they have a little depression or anxiety, a few more nightmares than normal. But they can cope. And they leave us alone." Her blob undulated from one shoulder to the other and she patted it gently. "The holidays are a perfect time to get them fed. So much frantic business, so many people out and about, so much stress. Loneliness."

"And a prime time for finding our newest members," Jolly Pants laughed and started to hum "Blue Christmas."

Blitzen danced behind him, swirling in sloppy circles under the shadows of the evergreen trees.

"Holidays are meant for family and friends, blah, blah blah," Gingersnap said, a rusty-blade edge to her voice that reminded me of Chase's tone whenever he talked about his uncle. "But really it just highlights the haves and the have-nots. Salt in the wound for the rest of us. You don't have to live like that anymore."

"How?" I asked.

"Like you, we come from broken homes," Gingersnap said, offering the shot glasses. "But our pets give us a home, together. And we have new creatures that need a host." She gestured to the two shot glasses, where the tiny blobs flexed and paused. Like they were waiting.

"What does it feel like?" I said after a minute and Chase yanked my shoulder.

"Are you *seriously* considering?" he hissed.

"What? Those things could make us freaking invincible," I whispered back. "Why not? This is a game-changer."

"Point. But…" Chase raised his voice.

"But what?" I asked. "You want to have a good Christmas for once, or what?"

"They live in your throat. You're still you. Just better." McMittens smiled her black-teeth smile and pursed her lips. "You can do what you want. Get back at who you want. And it doesn't hurt."

"Picture Stephan's face when we show up as a Macabre Elf. Picture your uncle," I said, and Chase grinned at last.

"Screw it." He reached for the shot, and we clinked glasses. "Merry Christmas to us."

Once more, we tipped back our heads and chugged.

THE PEERLINGS

Xenobiology - entry 210r

Never look at them.

We know they're coming from the buzzing. It starts an hour or so after what passes for sunset here scrawls its fluorescent yellow warning over the dunes.

We call them the Peerlings after our psychologist glimpsed a blur at her window before shutting her eyes out of fear. Something peered through the window, she said. Once the buzzing stopped, she forced herself to look. There was nothing to see: the Peerling was gone, and her husband had vanished. The first of many.

For almost ten years we lived on this new world in relative peace. We don't know why the Peerlings came, or why colonists started disappearing at the same time.

Extensive interviews of the survivors point to one perplexing conclusion: if you don't see the Peerlings, you don't get taken. Keeping your eyes closed, even if you hear them, somehow protects you.

A few colonists tried hitting or catching a Peerling with eyes shut but to no avail. Cameras fizzle when the Peerlings near. Even pulling a blanket or hat over your eyes isn't a foolproof safeguard; the Peerlings can make a sleep mask or sheet drop. The buzzing might resemble whispering at that point, hissing words that never fully form. But they drone on and on like an obsessive conviction your mind can't shake. But the one thing the Peerlings seem unable to do is force anyone's eyes open.

So at night, we all pretend to be asleep though we're far from it, willing ourselves not to peek as the buzzing intensifies. The curiosity almost kills you as much as the fear itself.

KAREN, the mayor, wasn't having any luck in stopping the bastards. She instituted a curfew so all the colonists were in bed, eye masks on, by sundown. But despite her precautions, people were still disappearing.

She had lost 46 people out of several hundred since the Peerlings made their first appearance three weeks prior. It had been a tough year; they had already lost a few souls to a violent stomach flu that had, at least, quickly run its course. Business as usual had ground to a halt, save for baseline processes and preparations for a contingency plan. Two scouting teams were investigating whether Peerlings showed up in various geographic regions around their colony. They needed potential relocation options, immediately.

As Karen passed from the housing structures toward their base, she overheard the geologist lecture to a small knot of people in the low morning light. He stood within the orb of a bulb hanging above the water storage shed. Even during mid-day, the planet never lit up more than a weak, salmon-colored glow from its nearby dimming sun, so they kept lights on throughout the day. But the atmosphere was livable, which was all that mattered.

"Humans do things even when they know they shouldn't," the geologist declared, shadows cascading along his grooved face. "The Peerlings show us we don't have willpower. Perhaps we do not deserve to be on this fresh new land. Perhaps we are being punished."

A few murmured in agreement and the geologist went on, emboldened as a small-town preacher, running a hand through his thinning hair. "Humans are inherently chaotic. We have no willpower. Witness our nonviable home planet."

Karen rolled her eyes and continued to the offices. All the colonists had been screened for mental stability before they left the habitat ships, but none of the hypothetical alien encounter scenarios they tested had anticipated what they were going through now.

Theirs was one of thousands of self-sufficient colonies that had scattered from the life ships to livable habitats once Earth was no longer an option. This planet wasn't a bad option—aside from the murky sunlight and stronger gravity than they were used to on the ships, it was a refreshing change. She had left an executive PR position at ForeverLight, an energy mining company that had flown no less than four ships.

Being mayor—even for only 500 people—had sounded like a good career shift at the time. The ships were never meant to be permanent homes. The change offered Karen the chance to start something new, something meaningful. But nothing in her extensive, crisis management training came close to preparing her for this disaster. Her team had calculated that, at this rate, their colony would dip below needed personnel levels for maintaining survival procedures in a mere month. They couldn't go back to Earth or the ships, and they didn't have the means to find another planet.

Two of her executive team were waiting in the lab, both with dark circles under their eyes.

"We have a new religious sect, it looks like," Karen said dryly as she perched on one of the stools. "Our geologist has become a Peerling prophet."

"He's a crackpot," Jazmine, the head of technology, said. "Can't weed them all out I suppose."

"I'll have to talk to him about it." Karen sighed. As if she didn't have enough to do.

"That reminds me of the early settlers in North America. They were strict but that mentality kept people alive in harsh environments," piped Omar, the engineering lead. "Irrational beliefs are hardwired. They help us clump together and impose order in the face of isolation and uncertainty. Karen, maybe it's best that they have an outlet."

Karen nodded slowly but Jazmine didn't look convinced.

"*Uncertainty*," Jazmine snorted. "I think you mean fatal invasion. If we're not careful the hive mind will turn into outright hysteria, and we'll be waging battle on two fronts."

"What have we got?" Karen said. Jazmine placed the exobiologist's report on the table. He disappeared last night while trying to observe the Peerlings from behind a barrier of protective eyewear and a suit helmet. They had told him it was a bad idea but he insisted. Said he couldn't go another night not knowing.

The team scanned his last recorded notes. Since anything electronic fizzled in the presence of the Peerlings, he had done it the old-fashioned way, erasable ink on a wipe-off board, typos and all.

> *Xenobiology entry 210w*
> > *face-to-face test*
> > *Testing physical shield. 1:05 am. Buzzing southwest. Higher frequency buzzing likely way of communicating (note—check with linguistic programs again). Louder but no physical indication of their presence. Lower temperature? (note—try thermometer next time) Louder now through helmet and earplugs. Buzzing buzzing. Saying something. Blur like ondensate*

That was the last of it. He had disappeared without a trace save for an empty helmet, the note board and a clean knife left in the murky morning sunlight.

Karen added him to her list for the next service. They had been holding services before breakfast every few days, once they had tallied the missing. During the brief speech, she recited the names of those gone, gave an update on progress and ended by reiterating their logo, "*The colony sticks together.*"

"Another piece of bad news," Jazmine said. "Despite our precautions, the rate of disappearance is unchanged."

Karen turned over the xenobiologist's board. "The scout teams should be back any day now. Relocating's going to be a bitch, but I don't think we have a choice. In case we need to buy more time, how is Plan B?"

"We should be ready to test it out in a few weeks," Omar said. He wasn't one for overselling, but his cautious optimism was promising. Omar's team seemed to think there was a way they could repurpose a decommissioned containment unit into an air-tight chamber to protect against the Peerlings. Karen didn't even know if they would be able to build enough for all the colonists but if the first one worked, at least it was something.

For the first time since the Peerlings arrived, she started to feel a bit better.

The sun glowed, enormous and orange-hued against the yellow sand dunes as Karen walked back toward her room. Never fully dark and never fully light, they were in a perpetual twilight that gave the merest hint of daytime and nighttime. Still, it was enough to set their circadian rhythms to, reinforced by the automated lighting schedule. Above, five other planets sprawled against the abyss like flecks of perfectly round paint spots on a black canvas.

"Karen!" someone called. "Wait!"

Karen turned as the head of security, Malcolm, approached. She favored him with a terse smile. They had slept together a few times, before the Peerlings had shown up. Since then, she slept alone, taking one of the limited sleeping pills they had to ensure she didn't wake throughout the night. The chemist had supplied the executive team with the last of the drugs, with the rationale that they had to remain functioning for the sake of the colony. The chemist was synthesizing more, but not fast enough.

"You look exhausted," Malcolm said, scratching his beard. "But I have good news. We just got a read on the east scouting crew's beacon. They should be within range tomorrow."

Karen perked up, but she knew better than to feel too hopeful. In the east sprawled a wide basin that they had identified early on as a possible location for a second base, if needed.

"What about the westbound team?" She asked. Crisis management was all about planning, backup plans, and *backups* for those plans. When she had worked for ForeverLight, countless fatalities and mining accidents taught her to operate in what she called "aggressive defensive" mode.

Malcolm shook his head. "No word from them yet."

Karen frowned. The western trail through the dried riverbeds was a faster route. They should've been back by now, or at least within comm range.

"How's your team's progress?" She had instructed security to set up automated motion-sensitive weaponry at night. So far, everything temporarily malfunctioned as soon as the Peerlings showed up.

"It's definitely some sort of electromagnetic interference," he said. "We're working on it."

Karen knew that "*we're working on it*" meant no good news. Malcolm's gaze searched hers and she sighed. She felt tired, bone-tired, despite the sleeping pills. He touched her elbow just as the curfew siren went off. She tilted her head toward the water shed, where the geologist's crowd grew despite the siren. "Make sure they get inside."

The next morning, Karen got word that a scout team was back.

Outside, she spotted only Xin, the eastbound team's field ops lead, next to the Rover, his shaved head bowed. Karen quickened her pace as Jazmine and Malcolm neared. She had sent a team of 10.

"All gone." Xin shuddered and closed his eyes. Malcolm and Jazmine exchanged a look.

"*All* of them?" Malcolm said.

"What happened exactly?" Jazmine said. "Tell us slowly."

"We went east to the basin, like we planned. Two weeks to the vantage point. But the first night we slept out there the sound was worse than anything I ever heard." He stabbed at his temple with his finger. "Like it was right inside your head. We lost two people the first night. Everyone else the second."

"Wait a minute—" Malcolm interrupted. "You were by yourself the entire time after that? How did you manage?"

"I started driving back the next morning. Heard them every night but nothing as bad as in the basin. We were easy pickings out there." His hoarse voice barely worked. Karen wondered if it was from screaming. She pictured the group in their sleeping bags, watching the alien sky turn into its strange purple dusk, half-dozing until the Peerlings approached. She grimaced, thinking of the bad news she'd have to deliver at tomorrow's service.

"It's worse out there," Xin continued and wiped his forehead. "I can't go again." His eyes fixed on Karen, and he very nearly pleaded. "Don't make me go out there again."

Karen looked at him steadily. "Malcolm, can you take Xin to medics and then meet in my office?"

She argued it out with Jazmine and the rest of the team for nearly an hour afterwards.

"We have to send out another scout team. There must be somewhere these things can't get to," Karen said. "Or somewhere they originate that we could target. The south range, maybe."

"Too treacherous," Malcolm said.

"We lost too many people," Jazmine said. "Sorry, Karen."

She was outvoted, so agreed to put it on the back burner for a few days. Someone knocked on the door, and Karen turned, irritated at the interruption until Omar burst in.

"I've got it," he huffed. It took him a second to catch his breath, but he was grinning.

Karen stood straighter. "What?"

"We were able to use a camera in a smaller version of the chamber as a proof of concept," Omar said. "Entirely sealed and locked. And it decreased interference from the Peerlings. Not prevented entirely but definitely decreased."

"Are you saying…" Malcolm held himself very still. "You recorded one of them?"

Omar pulled out his electronic pad. "It's not clear and it took me all day to calibrate it, but we definitely caught one. There, look."

The night camera's clip showed an empty room through a glass casing. The footage grew more staticky, almost impossible to see, as a buzzing grew deafening. But then—for the briefest second—something bobbed by, whitish. It looked like—

"A jellyfish," Jazmine said. "It kind of looks like an airborne jellyfish."

"Well, this rules out mass psychosis." Karen squinted at the screenshot. It had been one theory. "Are those tentacles?"

They rewound and watched the scraggly blob float by again but couldn't agree on definite features.

"Some sort of extraterrestrial life," Malcolm said finally. "Were you able to record anything else?"

Omar shook his head. "But this means the chamber should work on keeping out Peerlings. Possibly."

"Great job," Karen said. "We keep this confidential for now. Focus all your resources on finishing the chamber adaptation. It might be our only option at this point."

That night, even though her chemically induced sleep, images of out-of-focus jellyfish plagued Karen. The blurred figures reached out to her, whether in supplication or aggression, she couldn't tell.

The next day Karen was running late to the morning service. She straightened her ponytail and tried to blink the bleariness out of her eyes as she approached the town hall.

But something was wrong even before she got inside—another voice was speaking through the mic above shouts. Karen hurried through the open doors to see the geologist at her podium.

"Eyes are the windows to the soul!" The geologist was saying, a garland of facsimile skulls interspersed with the local graygrass swinging from his neck. A single strand of hair stuck up above his head, absurd under the artificial light. "And we are damned! They can see right into us and drag our immortal souls into hell."

Some of the crowd hollered back. "Damn straight!" "How do we repent?"

Karen pushed past dozens of shoulders, her eye catching strange, molded skull charms that a few of the colonists wore around their necks. She climbed the stairs to the platform, her eyes scanning for

Malcolm. He should have restored order, but he was nowhere to be seen. She pushed away a stab of worry as she faced the geologist.

"Herman, stop lying to these people," Karen snapped, facing the crowd beside him. She should have talked to him sooner, tried to reason with him without the audience, but it was too late now. She was good under pressure, with firm instincts taking hold and chasing away the last of her fatigue. "You're making everything worse by sprouting this babble." Her voice rang out loud and authoritative, and a few of the crowd turned toward her. "*The colony sticks together.* And you're breaking us apart."

"I've seen them!" Herman screamed and Karen froze as the crowd grew hushed. She had kept Omar's video strictly confidential.

Smugly, Herman continued. "I've seen the Peerlings!"

Someone shouted: "What do they look like?" and someone else: "how did you survive?"

"They came to me in a dream," Herman said, and Karen rolled her eyes, breathing easy again. "They are angels from above and devils from below, seeking revenge for our wrongs. We have to repent. It's the only way to save our colony."

"In a *dream*? Do you even hear yourself?" Karen snorted and flicked the strange garland around his neck. "And what the hell is that? Clay skulls? Morbid, really."

He jerked back, the rogue hair pointing up like an arrow. "There's nothing wrong with showing your faith to the Peerlings." He turned back to the audience. "They'll know who is who. Who is the true believer, and who is not."

"Enough!" Malcolm shouted, breaking through the crowd. Karen felt a sweep of relief—the Peerlings hadn't gotten him.

Herman glared and marched off the stage. Over the crowd's muttering, Karen gave her usual introduction to the service and read the list of names Malcolm provided her with. Half a dozen, plus the nine from the scouting mission. The faces below her grew stormier and stormier. Immediately after, Karen called another team meeting to brainstorm new solutions, to no avail.

At sunset and bone tired, Karen set out her usual preparations:

blindfold, earplugs, a fragment of her last sleeping pill. It wasn't more than an hour later she jolted out of her restless sleep.

The pill had worn off far too early.

A low buzzing was enough to make her stiffen and press a clammy hand over her blindfold. It had been days since she had heard the Peerlings thanks to the pills. She had forgotten how horrible the sound was, droning on like a giant insect and intensifying by the wall on her left, as if something succeeded in burrowing through.

Through her mask, she sensed the remaining light flicker and go dark, plunging her into an even inkier blackness.

To distract herself from the fear that was starting to set in, Karen mentally recited the alphabet backwards. The high-pitched humming slinked around her room, from left to right and back again. She wiped off the sweat drenching the back of her neck and jammed the earplugs further in.

No change. It was like the buzzing was inside her head.

Karen tried not to think about the translucent thing she had seen on the screen, its pixelated tentacles waving like something underwater. Instead, she grabbed her pillow and started swinging. The thought of making contact with the straggly form was almost as bad as not.

"What do you want? What the hell do you want?" Karen meant to say but shrieked it instead. She stopped swinging and, shivering, held still until the sound finally, *mercifully*, subsided, disappearing the way it had come.

The colony never did hear anything from the westbound scout team.

That morning, the geologist was hanging, very publicly, above the stage in the town hall. Karen hadn't seen it herself, but it was easy enough to imagine Herman swaying like a bent stalk, his dark eyes wide and blank, clay skulls floating softly from his neck.

Someone from Malcolm's early shift had spotted the body and cut it down before most of the colonists were up. The damage was done though. Everyone knew by breakfast.

There had only been one suicide in their ten-year history, and it happened shortly after the ship dropped them off. A young man—he would have been Karen's age by now—couldn't take being landside and desperately wanted to return to space, even though it was a one-way trip. Pietr. Karen recalled his name, even now.

At Jazmine's urging, Karen called an emergency service. The colonists gathered, not quite mob-like but with their anger simmering just below the surface, ready to break at any moment. Worse yet, one or two shot suspicious glances her way.

Malcolm's team had clearly identified the case as a suicide. Karen's mind had already gone to the worse-case scenario: a rumor gaining traction that it was a political murder, particularly after her very public confrontation with the geologist. She needed to give them a bone, and fast.

"We have a plan," Karen announced as she swept up to the podium, ignoring Jazmine's startled glance. She didn't know exactly what she would say until she said it, but her words always flowed easily and with conviction, which was half the battle. "We haven't mentioned this before now because the relocation was our primary objective, but our incredible engineering team has designed a device that may protect us from the Peerlings."

Murmurs rose and swept through the crowd, and she gestured to Omar in the front, who looked stunned. She didn't like catching her team off guard, but these were desperate times. "Our head of engineering will tell you more." After a moment Omar jogged up the stage next to her.

"It's a repurposed contamination unit," he said to the crowd. "Locked against air contaminants and other physical toxins, it may potentially keep out the Peerlings."

Most of the muttering had died down, and a few colonists were listening attentively.

Karen took the mic once more. "We are doing the first test tonight. You are all welcome to come to the lab before sundown to see the set-up."

Omar's eyes grew wide and Jazmine's stare from the audience was laser-intense. Someone in the crowd applauded, followed by others. Karen didn't let her relief show but kept her jaw firm and her eyes focused as she shouted their rallying cry, "*The colony sticks together!*" The applause rose and a few cheers broke out as some echoed the cry back to her.

"Is the unit even ready yet?" Jazmine hissed once they had barely closed the doors to Karen's office.

"It's going to have to be," Malcolm said grimly. "Or you risk a riot."

"I had a lot more testing I need to do—" Omar began.

"But it's close enough?" Karen interjected.

"It's close enough," he repeated, though he looked uncharacteristically frazzled. "But we need to do a lot more tests before trying it out with a human."

"We shouldn't rush this," Jazmine said. "And we'll need to select the subject carefully. It'll basically be a suicide mission."

"I'm doing it," Karen said, and the rest were silent for a split second before protesting. She held up a hand. "I have to. Before I worked for ForeverLight I was at a small food preservation company. When we had an outbreak of listeria—hitting 6 full ships—we very nearly had a mob situation on our hands. People were starving but everyone was afraid to eat the new batch. Do you know how I handled that?" Karen looked at her team, all of whom stared steadily back at her. Cautious, afraid. But trusting. They trusted her and she was going to see this through.

She continued. "I broadcast myself eating a full food pak, picked at random by one of the most vocal critics. It was a stunt, but it was authentic. It dissipated everyone's fears more effectively than anything else I could have done. We're about to lose control of the whole colony and this will regain their trust. We can't risk anarchy or we're dead, simple as that."

Omar looked thoughtful and Jazmine's brow was furrowed. Malcolm was the only one who looked entirely unconvinced, but Karen didn't give him a chance to chime in.

"It'll work, I'm sure of it. Sunset's just around the corner." Karen opened her office door. "Let's hustle."

"This is a terrible idea," Malcolm said again as Karen zipped up one of their decontamination suits. It was a bulky fit, but she folded her sleeves and tucked the sagging pant legs into her boots. While a suit alone hadn't provided protection for the exobiologist, they figured the more barriers between her and the Peerlings, the better.

"We're out of time. If it works, we can start constructing units for the whole colony. It will take a lot of resources but it's the only option we have right now." She was careful not to look directly in Malcolm's eyes. If she did, and spotted the hint of fear she was sure was there, she might lose her nerve.

Malcolm shifted from one foot to the other, not quite pacing but holding back an agitated energy that might all but yank her out of there.

Before he could do anything like that, Karen stepped into the glass chamber. The unit was meant for containment of one or two adults should they encounter any infections that needed quarantine. It was like being in a fishbowl, with room for a cot.

The unit rested in a cleared-out section of the lab storage area next to the observation room. Her team would be on the other side of the observation glass with a mic and recording equipment. They fully expected the equipment to fizzle again, but Jazmine insisted they try.

Dozens of colonists packed into the observation room, talking amongst themselves as they stared down through the glass.

"What are you going to do, open your eyes as soon as you hear them?" Malcolm said to her from outside the chamber. "It's not going to work."

"We have to see if it's safe. If bacteria can't get in here, I don't see how they will." Karen did look at Malcolm now, and the worry line that creased his brow gave her pause. "This is the best option." She said the words as confidently as she could, but the crease only deepened.

Omar hurried over and pointed to a small set of dials and a screen. "Final tests on the air filters and life support are all set. You can talk to us through here. I don't know how long it will last once the Peerlings show up, but if the cam was any indication, all the tech will be in and out for a bit. The cameras in there with you are on auto with local backups and streams to us, so hopefully we can see whatever you see before they cut out. Good luck, Karen."

Jazmine knocked against the glass. "It's go time. You can handle this, I know you can."

Malcolm was harder to see off as Omar sealed the door.

"If anything starts to go wrong, close your eyes and holler, OK?" he said before it closed.

"Piece of cake." Karen smiled.

Malcolm's team cleared the observation room and readied cots and blindfolds for the management group. Karen perched, trying to ignore the scratchiness of her suit and the heaviness of her helmet. She felt as she always did under pressure: alert but calm. Excited even, at the thought of finally figuring out what these damn things were.

Though the sun had just set, the lab storage area was brightly lit. She glanced up at the observation window, where her team reclined, blindfolded, waiting.

"All good?" Karen said through the mic and settled herself back against the cot, forcing her eyes closed.

"All—" Omar's voice started when it cut out and back in. "Good. Karen?"

"Can you hear me?"

Static answered her. The Peerlings were there.

Karen strained her ears—there, she could just barely hear it, the faintest buzz. It's now or never, she thought, her heart pounding. She cracked one eye and took a moment to adjust to the light inside her chamber. She almost yelled out in joy. The chamber was *working*—she was protected. And could *see*.

There was a single Peerling, floating like a grotesque, translucent microbe or shrimp, magnified to human size, outside of her chamber. The room, save for the light next to her and up in the observation area, had dimmed, electronics flickering off in the Peerling's presence.

It turned. A scream tried to work its way out of Karen's throat but dried up as she gasped.

The Peerling had *eyes. Horrible* eyes. Three human-like irises burrowed into her, causing a hum to strike up within her body. The buzzing differentiated itself into words:

"Help us," the Peerling said. Its voice didn't sound remotely human even though Karen could understand it. It sounded like a swarm of bees trying to talk.

So they were sentient and communicative lifeforms. Karen didn't lose a beat and prayed that the equipment was recording some of this.

"What are you?" she said carefully but firmly, while continuing to keep eye contact. She had to make it clear that they weren't prey to be picked off, even though its irises made her want to cower. "What do you want from us? Perhaps we can work together if you tell me."

Never in a million years would she have guessed what it said next.

"We are you."

Karen started to shiver, her skin bunched and tender despite her suit. "What do you mean? That doesn't make sense. Try again."

"Colonists," the Peerling buzzed, and the containment unit felt far too small to Karen, so small she wondered if she was getting enough breathable air. She didn't want the Peerling to talk anymore, not to say another word.

Its buzzing continued. "Stuck. Atmosphere holds. Earth-like but not Earth. Sky like a wall. Won't let us go. Need to go."

Karen practically laughed, it was so absurd. But something about the Peerling's three-iris gaze looked familiar and sent a shiver down her spine. Her body started to vibrate again. She shook it off and focused. "*Where* do you need to go?"

"Need you." The Peerling seemed agitated, flickering like an apparition. "More colonists, go further. Critical mass. Close. Escape atmosphere. Weren't meant to be here. Trapped. Can't go where we need to go. Need to go."

The geologist's words came back to her unbidden: *Eyes are the windows to the soul.*

"Like where, heaven? Hell?" The words seemed to dry up in Karen's mouth. "They aren't real."

"We don't know. *Need to go.*" Its agitation had turned to urgency, to a demand.

Karen had never been religious, but now an unwanted image popped up of her soul being wrenched out of her body by the Peerling.

"So what, are you like ghosts? Of our—" She couldn't finish the thought and instead glanced up at the observation glass. Her team was sitting but still blindfolded, Omar pushing at his control panel and Jazmine's mouth moving. Malcolm was blindly pounding on the glass.

"If you were once here with us, Pietr, Herman, whoever you are, why would you pick us off like this? Why would you *murder* us?"

"*The colony sticks together,*" the Peerling said. "*The colony sticks together.* Need to go."

Other Peerlings had appeared, three dozen at least, together in a white cloud pushing against the wall of her chamber. If she counted them—and she *wouldn't*, she *couldn't* face the idea just yet—it might be the number of colonists that had died since they landed.

The buzzing from the Peerlings grew louder, coaxing her cells to hum in unison. Not just hum—but rupture. A word came to her: *evanesce.* They were forcing her to evanesce and become like them. Some of the Peerlings clouded the observation glass above, which had gone dark, and Karen hoped her colleagues kept their eyes shut.

A wisp of translucent material coalesced in front of her and the temperature in her suit dropped ten degrees. The light in her chamber blinked and went out. Karen closed her eyes as the Peerling that had spoken to her took full shape inside the chamber.

"Mayor," it buzzed.

She began to come apart, unravel like a badly made sweater. Karen clenched her teeth and eyelids and hoped that at least some of the equipment had recorded something, to warn the others.

Her eyelids were cold, tugging, pouring. The world around her materialized as both sharp and multiplexed, as though she were looking through a diamond. She felt the beginnings of a massive, nameless pressure overhead and a distance so far and so wrong it wracked her with vertigo. They were too far, they would never make it back to their tether, to the core that collected them once their bodies failed. The cycle was blocked, this world was not for them.

They had made a horrible mistake.

She had one last thought, or really, realization, before she fully dissipated:

Everyone opens their eyes in the end.

ACKNOWLEDGMENTS

First, a huge thanks to Dragon's Roost Press for publishing this collection and to the Horror Writers Association (HWA)'s annual Stokercon event, where I had a chance to meet Michael Cieslak and pitch this book. And thank you to Luke Spooner of Carrion House for doing a fabulous job on the cover.

My endless gratitude goes to friends and members of the energetic indie horror community who have supported me along the way. Thanks in particular to the editors who took a chance on my work, including Bruce Bethke, Jeremy Billingsley, Mike Davis, Alex Ebenstein, Eddie Generous, Alex Hofelich, Rebecca Rowland, Kristi Petersen Schoonover, Sara Tantlinger, Trevor Williamson, and many others.

Critical readers help make stories shine, so I am deeply appreciative to those who gave feedback for some of these tales way back when: Henry Herz, Moaner T. Lawrence, Donna J. W. Munro, Frank Wu, and others. Their feedback has made my stories stronger. A special shoutout to my San Diego HWA group, especially Dennis K. Crosby, Sarah Faxon and Theresa Halvorsen.

And, as always, thanks to my family: my dad for introducing us to fantasy, sci-fi, and horror when we were kids; my mom for saying she likes my writing better than Stephen King's; my sister for being my frantic proofreader under short deadlines; my partner for being a steady presence on this rollercoaster of careers and parenthood; and my two little wildlings for keeping me on my toes.

PUBLICATION HISTORY

"Vermin" was first published in *Unnerving Magazine*.

"Gifting" is original to this collection.

"All Aboard" was first published in *34 Orchard Magazine*.

"Terror on the Boulevard" is original to this collection.

"Just Another Apocalypse" was first published by Rooster Republic Press.

"What Storms Bring" was first published in the *Lovecraft eZine*.

"The Color of Friendship" was first published in *Chromophobia: A Strangehouse Anthology by Women in Horror*.

"Lonely Arcade" was first published in *Stupefying Stories*.

"The Sighting" was first published in *Stupefying Stories*.

"The U Train" was first published by Sley House Publishing.

"Perfect Gift" is original to this collection.

"Unrest" was first published in *Dancing in the Shadows: A Tribute to Anne Rice*.

"The Night Call" was first published by Gypsum Sound Tale's *Colp* magazine.

"Better Halves" was first published in the *Lovecraft eZine*.

"From Sea to Shining Sea" was first published in *Field Notes From a Nightmare*.

Publication History

"Blessed" was first published by Sley House Publishing.

"The Circus King" was first published in *Typehouse Literary Magazine*.

"Puddle of Comradely Despair" is original to this collection.

"Macabre Elves" is original to this collection.

"The Peerlings" was first published in *Beyond the Infinite: Tales from the Outer Reaches*.

ABOUT THE AUTHOR

KC Grifant is an award-winning writer based in Southern California who creates internationally published horror, fantasy, science fiction, and weird west stories. Many of her short stories have appeared in podcasts, magazines, games, and Stoker-nominated anthologies.

Her weird western novel, *Melinda West: Monster Gunslinger* (Brigids Gate Press, 2023), described as a blend of Bonnie & Clyde meet *The Witcher* and *Supernatural*, is the first in a series. It ranked #1 in Amazon New Releases for Western Horrors and has received positive reviews internationally. She is also co-creator of the *Monster Gunslingers* card game.

In addition to writing, she is the co-chair and founder of the Horror Writers Association San Diego chapter, a short story instructor, and member of numerous writing organizations, including the Science Fiction and Fantasy Writers Association. In between her day job as a nonfiction science communicator, she chases two small children and drinks far too much coffee.

Learn more at www.KCGrifant.com or connect on the social networks at @KCGrifant.

ALSO BY KC GRIFANT

Melinda West: Monster Gunslinger (Brigids Gate Press, 2023)

When monsters roam the Old West, there is one gunslinging couple who can tilt the odds in favor of humanity.

Stoic sharpshooter Melinda and her easygoing partner Lance are pros at fighting everything from giant flying scorpions to psychic bugs. But when they accidentally release a demon that steals souls, they find themselves caught in a supernatural war. Melinda and Lance must battle a menagerie of monsters and hunt a notorious outlaw to save their friends and stop hell on Earth.

Melinda West and the Gremlin Queen (Brigids Gate Press, 2025)

Monster exterminators Melinda and Lance are forced back into action when a new breed of creatures begin hunting humans in the Old West. The gremlins are stronger and faster than any monster before them—and more intelligent. Melinda and Lance must stop the invasion of near-indestructible, bloodthirsty gremlins before they lose everyone they love.

Praise for Melinda West: Monster Gunslinger

"This fun, imaginative, and confident series opener will be a massive crowd pleaser for general audiences, especially for those who enjoy a wide range of popular weird western offerings."

— LIBRARY JOURNAL

"KC Grifant's horror western hits the road at top speed and never takes its foot off the accelerator, making the book a perfect fit for readers who like their horror weird and their action plentiful. Grifant's heroine is a delicious amalgamation of Ash Williams in wise-cracking bravado and Ellen Ripley in triumphant fearlessness…I found myself putting off going to sleep each night just so I could continue onto the next chapter."

— GINGER NUTS OF HORROR

"Powerfully imaginative... with action and enjoyable monsters. Terrific action scenes ensue as a result and the action ramps up to the end."

— HORROR DNA

"KC Grifant comes out guns blazing with MELINDA WEST: MONSTER GUNSLINGER –a devious action-packed adventure set in a very weird version of the Old West. Fast, furious, and a hell of a lot of fun!"

— JONATHAN MABERRY, NY TIMES BESTSELLING AUTHOR OF *SON OF THE POISON ROSE* AND *RELENTLESS*

"Melinda West is the hero I've been waiting for as long as I can remember. The world and characters are vivid and magical. This story is a delight."

— KATE JONEZ, BRAM STOKER AND SHIRLEY JACKSON AWARD-NOMINATED AUTHOR

"Grifant writes with a deft hand, giving us compulsive prose and an easy feeling for her storytelling. I found I was utterly shocked at how much book I was devouring and how quickly...Grifant is a powerfully imaginative author who paints cinematic pictures easily with her descriptions and will make you feel the dust and smell the gunpowder time and time again."

— STEVE STRED, SPLATTERPUNK-NOMINATED AUTHOR OF *SACRAMENT, MASTODON* AND *CHURN THE SOIL*

"I've been absolutely riveted to the story KC weaved, and adored everything about it. Imagine Supernatural's hunting ... combined with the most badass female lead you can imagine, amazing supporting characters, nail-biting suspense, great action, and the grunge and grit you expect in a Western."

— TASHA REYNOLDS, HORROR REVIEWER AND HOST OF THE GHOULISH GALLERY PODCAST

DRAGON'S ROOST PRESS

Dragon's Roost Press is the fever dream brainchild of dark speculative fiction author Michael Cieslak. Since 2014, their goal has been to find the best speculative fiction authors and share their work with the public. For more information about Dragon's Roost Press and their publications, please visit:

http://www.thedragonsroost.biz

Made in the USA
Middletown, DE
19 September 2024

60698460R00116